Death in the West End

London Cosy Mysteries
Book 2

Rachel McLean

Millie Ravensworth

ACKROYD
PUBLISHING

Copyright © 2023 by Rachel McLean and Millie Ravensworth

All rights reserved.

No part of this book may be reproduced in any form or by any electronic or mechanical means, including information storage and retrieval systems, without written permission from the author, except for the use of brief quotations in a book review.

This is a work of fiction. Names, characters, businesses, places, events and incidents are either the products of the author's imagination or used in a fictitious manner. Any resemblance to actual persons, living or dead, or actual events is purely coincidental.

Ackroyd Publishing

ackroyd-publishing.com

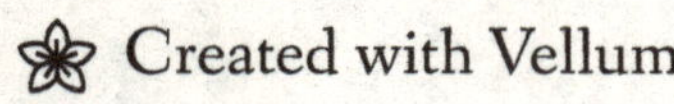 Created with Vellum

Death in the West End

Chapter One

"My Fair Lady," said Zaf Williams, sitting in an armchair in the foyer of London's Redhouse Hotel.

"Oliver!" said Penny from behind the reception desk.

"Miss Saigon."

"Jesus Christ Superstar."

"Matilda."

"Mamma Mia!"

"Les Mis."

"Phantom of the Opera."

"I always had a soft spot for Mary Poppins," said Diana Bakewell, approaching the reception desk across the luxurious foyer carpet.

"Did you now?" Zaf eyed the duck-headed umbrella his fellow tour guide carried under her arm.

"I meant the Sherman Brothers songs as much as anything," Diana replied. "Are we listing our favourite musicals?"

"We're still waiting for our American guests to emerge," said Penny.

Zaf looked along the corridor to the restaurant and the lifts. Chartwell and Crouch tours had been engaged to spend the week escorting an investment team from New York between various locations. The team were in London to finalise a deal that would see a West End musical travel to Broadway. Zaf's understanding was that the week was to be half business, half London sightseeing.

"Do the Americans love Britain so much that they have to come over here and buy up our musicals?" he asked.

"They love the *idea* of Britain, perhaps," said Diana. "And maybe we should be grateful that British creativity is still a sought-after commodity."

Zaf looked through the goody bags arranged beside the reception desk and pulled out a glossy flyer for the Delphinium Theatre.

"*The Cockney's Complaint*. Never heard of it."

"*Voices of History*," Penny said. "You've heard that song."

"The Adele song? That's from this?" Zaf looked up, impressed.

"Musicals are big business," Diana said. "Ask me

how much profit *Cats* has made since it debuted on the West End in nineteen eighty-one."

Zaf gave her a tired look. Diana was nearly three times his age and seemed to have spent her life in London soaking up random trivia. At times, it felt like there wasn't a single London-related fact she didn't know.

He took a deep breath. "Diana, tell me how much money *Cats* has made since—"

"Look lively." Diana pointed down the corridor.

A dozen people, some in suits, some less formal, were emerging from the restaurant. A young woman with her hair in a bun strode ahead, consulting an open document wallet. Judging by her tight, fast stride, Zaf imagined she was a PA or a tour manager or something like that.

She gave Penny a knowing look: *yeah, definitely a PA*.

"Brie, Zaf, Diana," said Penny. "Diana, Zaf, Brie."

"Good morning," Diana said. She turned from the PA to the rest of the group. "Morning, everyone."

The group looked at her with blank faces and tired eyes.

"I hope you enjoyed your breakfast," said Zaf. The Redhouse breakfasts were amazing; he could smell the fresh coffee and buttery pastries from here.

"Honey," said a woman with shiny caramel-coloured hair, "they could have given me the finest breakfast of my life, and I'd have barely tasted it." She placed a hand on his arm. "The jetlag has left me reeling."

"Sounds terrible," he agreed.

"Oh, you're sweet," she replied.

Diana gestured to the goody bags. "Please, help yourselves to a gift bag. Courtesy of the Delphinium Theatre. And then I'll show you to your transport for the day."

A few of the party picked up bags; the rest, too bleary-headed to notice, walked on out of the hotel. Zaf scooped up the remaining bags and followed the party outside where a red double-decker bus waited for them. As he caught up with the Americans, he caught a familiar waft of vanilla and almond and wrinkled his nose, unable to place it.

"Take a seat wherever you'd like," said Diana from the open entrance at the back by the spiral stairs, "upstairs or downstairs."

"Riding in style, I see," grunted a man. He was lean, with possibly the thinnest head Zaf had ever seen.

"Mr Romano," said the PA, Brie, "the good people at the Delphinium wanted you to see the real London. There's no better way to do that than from the seat of a red London bus."

"Tell that to my chiropractor." Mr Romano sniffed and stepped onto the bus.

Zaf hadn't worked with many Americans before; his fellow students at uni studying Art History had been mostly Brits, and growing up in Birmingham hadn't exactly been a cosmopolitan experience. But even he could hear a difference in the accents. The pencil-thin Mr Romano sounded like he had just stepped out of a yellow New York taxi, but Brie's accent was barely American at all.

Mr Romano stamped the wooden slats of the floor. "This bus is old?"

Zaf noticed Diana's wince.

"We get a lot of positive feedback from customers about our beautiful vintage Routemaster bus." She waved him down the aisle. "They aren't in everyday service now, but our buses are well cared for and boast original mid-twentieth century features."

"Nineteen fifty-seven chassis," called the driver, Newton Crombie, from the front of the bus.

"*Old* old," Mr Romano whispered.

Zaf smiled at Brie. "This looks like a fun bunch."

"Work with them," she said. "Work with them and see if you wouldn't want to murder them all after the first week."

Brie held out a takeaway cup to the caramel-haired woman as she climbed into the bus. "I snagged you a cup of black coffee, Serena."

Serena, elegant in a purple silk blouse and tailored trousers, rolled her eyes. "I've only got one pair of hands, Brie. How am I supposed to manage this goody bag as well as a coffee?"

Brie held out her hand for the gift bag and Serena

took her coffee. She followed Mr Romano further into the bus, leaving Brie with two gift bags and folders tucked under her arm.

"Need a hand?" Zaf asked.

"I'm used to it," said the not-quite-American.

"You haven't murdered her yet."

"What? Serena McNash? Director of the Kenosha Falls Organization, owner of three Broadway theatres? Tony-winning Serena McNash, the woman who pays my wages?"

Zaf shrugged: he'd never heard of half those things.

Brie stepped on board, then turned to him. "You don't kill the golden goose, Zaf." She lowered her voice to a whisper. "At least, not until you've got all the gold."

Zaf stepped onto the bus, catching that scent of vanilla and almond again. Brie's perfume, perhaps? Serena's? The croissants from the hotel? He wasn't sure.

Chapter Two

The bus pulled away from the hotel. Diana took the microphone as they got underway.

"Welcome to our tour bus. Chartwell and Crouch tours will be at your service for your stay this week. This morning we'll be taking you on an introductory sightseeing tour, to welcome you to London from the United States."

The slender New Yorker, Mr Romano, turned in his seat, searching for something.

"Lost something there?" Diana asked.

He turned to her. "Seatbelt?"

She shook her head. *Not on a vintage Routemaster.*

"Don't they have rules over here about vehicle safety?"

"Reuben." Serena waved her coffee at him. "We

talked about this. England is a perfectly safe place to be."

"We do have rules," said Diana. "But you don't tend to find seatbelts on this sort of bus."

Serena's gaze met Diana's. "New accountant. Un-travelled is an understatement."

"I've travelled," snapped Reuben.

Serena raised an eyebrow. "Long weekends in Montauk do not count as travelling."

The party, almost all of them downstairs, were staring out at the scenery. Even the unremarkable parts of Baker Street and then the Marylebone Road drew points and comments. That was the beauty of travel, Diana supposed. The ordinary became extraordinary.

A few of the group were sifting through their gift bags. Diana had inspected their contents at the hotel; it would have been generous to describe them as eclectic.

There was a bottle of London Pride beer, a bottle opener shaped like a Coldstream Guard, a phrasebook of 'authentic' Cockney phrases and a box of 'Original London Soap'. Someone, either in the Delphinium marketing team or maybe in a back office of Chartwell and Crouch tours, had been told to make the gifts London-themed.

Serena pulled something soft and fluffy from her bag.

"I appear to have a rat in a red felt hat."

Diana smiled. "It's a Paddington Bear toy. Not the best likeness."

"Oh, I like Paddington Bear," Brie said.

"The Paddington author, Michael Bond, lived in Paddington, just north of here," Diana said.

"Oh, it's real?" Reuben looked surprised.

"The place," Diana told him. "Not the bear."

"Are we going there today?"

She shook her head. "This is as far north as we're going today."

The bus continued past the green expanse of Hyde Park towards Buckingham Palace, the Thames and, after a bit of sightseeing to-and-fro, their planned destination: the Delphinium, in the heart of Theatreland.

Chapter Three

As they approached the rear of Buckingham Palace and Zaf prepared to pick up the mic, he caught the scent of vanilla and almond again. He turned to Diana.

"Diana, can I ask you something?"

"Is this about how much money *Cats* has made?"

"Have you been using my vanilla and almond body cream?"

She blinked at him. "The handwash in the little bottle by the sink?"

"You have!"

She sniffed the back of her hand. "It's very nice."

"I know. It's mine. I..."

Zaf had been living in London for less than a year, and his domestic situation had been chaotic to say the least. Rental prices, even for single rooms, were astronomical, and Zaf had lurched from one dodgy situation to another until Diana had offered to let him stay in her apartment. Temporarily.

Temporary had gone from days to weeks. The flat, a third of a house in Eccleston Square, was huge, but that that still didn't make it easy.

"Shall I buy some soap for the bathroom?" he suggested.

"Even more products?"

Zaf bristled: was that a criticism?

"If you like," he said, keeping his voice level. "That body cream's expensive."

"Or you could buy some of the groceries on the list on the fridge."

"I'll do that."

"They say that two can live as cheaply as one," Diana said.

"They do." Zaf wasn't so sure.

Diana frowned. "Three and a half billion pounds."

"What?"

"*Cats*," she said. "The musical. It's made three and a half billion. Musical theatre's big business."

"Wow. Everyone likes cats, I s'pose."

"And we need to keep these people happy." She eyed the tour group.

I can take a hint, Zaf thought.

He grabbed the mic and performed his best tour guide spiel all the way past Buckingham Palace, along Birdcage Walk and across Westminster Bridge. Once

Newton was on the south side of the river, he looped round to cross back over on the Waterloo Bridge, and Zaf handed the mic to Diana.

"We'll cross over the river again, to give you a different perspective," she explained. "The London Eye is on your immediate left, and as we approach the other bank, you can see Somerset House on the right. It's been in some films, including *Love Actually* and *Goldeneye*.

"On the left-hand side we see Victoria Embankment, and if you look carefully, you can see Cleopatra's Needle."

"How old would that be?" asked Reuben.

Diana nodded. "It's thousands of years old."

"Thousands of years? Amazing. Is there a lot of really old stuff here in London?"

"London is a fabulously layered city," Diana replied. "It's been here since Roman times and you can find nuggets of history from every era between then and the modern age. But Cleopatra's Needle only came to London in the nineteenth century."

"Did you say the *Romans* lived here?" Reuben breathed. "That's amazing. I'm a Romano, so... You see?"

"I see."

"Are there any still here?" The accountant looked excited.

"Are there any *Romans* still here?" Diana took a deep breath. "When I describe something as Roman, I mean that it dates from the Roman Empire. Around two thousand years ago."

Reuben nodded and peered out of the window.

Serena called over. "Unworldly is not the word to describe this man."

"Hey," he said.

"Hey yourself, bud." She looked at Diana. "He's a smart guy, really. You've got to be to crunch all those numbers, huh? But really, Rube by name..."

Diana smiled. She wasn't about to get involved. "If you're interested in Roman ruins, there's a temple to Mithras off Cannon Street."

"Cat!" someone shouted.

Diana turned to see the bus cat, Gus, sitting on the spiral steps.

Gus was a round cat, just the right side of fat. His fur shifted from brown to silver to grey, depending on the light. Since adopting Chartwell and Crouch as his home he'd cast himself as some sort of tour bus mascot.

When a new group joined them, Gus would sound them out. He had an instinct for the people who'd let him sit on their laps, and possibly even give him the good bits out of their sandwiches.

"Is that a cat?" Serena asked.

"It's Gus," Diana said. "He's an unofficial member of the crew. Are you not much of a cat person?"

"I live for cats! I had to leave my own fur babies with a carer and I miss them every day. What breed is

Gus?" Serena reached for Gus, who strolled up the aisle and arched his back under her hand.

"I'm not sure he has a breed," said Diana. "He's just a regular tabby cat."

Serena tried to get Gus to sit on her lap. He obliged for a moment, then sprang up onto Brie's lap, wrapping his paws around the fluffy Paddington Bear souvenir from the gift bag.

Brie's eyes were wide. "He thinks it's a rat in a hat, too."

Serena pulled out her own toy and waggled it at Gus. He leapt across the aisle towards it. Immediately a half dozen more were waved at him.

Diana sighed. The sights and sounds of one of the most thrilling capitals of the world were right outside, and here they all were, enthralled by a tabby cat. Even if it was her favourite tabby cat.

Chapter Four

As the Routemaster bus drew up along Coventry Street in the heart of London's West End, there were still more eyes on Gus the cat than on the scenery. Two hours travelling through London culture, and history had been upstaged by a moggy.

Gus sat on Brie's lap. Serena had shifted over to stroke his fur as she gazed out of the window. Zaf wondered if Serena had encouraged him to sit on someone else's lap to protect her designer trousers.

"And here we are," said Diana, "the Delphinium Theatre, home to the hit musical, *The Cockney's Complaint.*"

Some people were immediately on their feet. Others were more sluggish.

"My body can't work out if it's morning or night," said the Broadway accountant, Reuben.

"Did you do all the things I told you to avoid jet-lag?" Serena asked. She picked a cat hair off her knee before standing.

"Like drinking all the alcohol the flight attendants offered me? I'm not sure that helped, to be honest."

Serena's mouth dropped open. "I said *don't* drink all the alcohol they offer you! Seriously. You must be so dehydrated."

Reuben's face was a picture of dawning comprehension. He looked like he was about to say something, but thought better of it.

Brie spoke up. "We can get you something alcohol-free at the drinks reception in the theatre, Reuben. If you'd like?"

Reuben shrugged. He'd saturated himself so thoroughly in free drinks that it probably made no difference.

Zaf guided everyone off the bus and observed their reactions to London's West End. Theatreland was chock-a-block with theatres and restaurants. The theatre opposite had a poster for the musical *Dick!*. The two leads, Dick Whittington and his human-sized cat, were pictured leaning back-to-back, obliterated by a 'cancelled' sign.

Zaf waved to Newton as the doors closed and the bus drew away. The driver would be back later for the return journey to the hotel, but Zaf and Diana would stay with the Americans for their drinks reception.

On the pavement, Serena leaned over to him. "You're going to look after us well, I can tell." She winked and passed him a fifty-pound note.

Zaf stared at it in his hand, both fascinated and horrified. He'd never seen a fifty-pound note before. He'd heard that Americans liked to tip, but this...

"I can't take this."

"You can and you will," Serena told him. "I'm impressed with your vigour."

The theatre foyer was like most of the original theatres in this part of London, posh twirly architecture mixed with a gaudy fairground look. They probably went through a lot of gold-coloured paint whenever they had to refresh the place, Zaf thought.

Diana winked at the woman behind the glass in the box office, and Zaf shook his head: another of her acquaintances.

A movement caught his eye and he glanced backwards.

Something had run into the theatre and disappeared. Something... grey?

He put a hand on Diana's arm, causing her to flinch. She was still annoyed with him about the toiletries.

"Did you see something?" he asked. "Has Gus come in here with us?"

She looked around the foyer. "We'd have seen him get off the bus."

A woman stepped forward to greet the group. She was poised and elegant in a silk dress, her dark hair pinned up.

"Hello, everybody. I'm Charlotte Webber, the theatre manager here at the Delphinium. I'd like to formally welcome you all to our beautiful theatre. We have a lunch and drinks reception waiting." Her voice was clipped, robotic even: it was clear she did this a lot.

Zaf turned back to the group. He'd been imagining things, and besides, there wasn't time to check.

Charlotte Webber was greeting the visitors one by one, shaking hands and introducing herself again and again. Zaf blinked as she grabbed his hand.

"You're part of the charm offensive too." She winked at him.

Zaf wasn't sure what to say. Diana would have a better answer, he was sure.

Charlotte turned to the group. "If you would all follow me, we'll go through to the backstage area where we've set up some hospitality."

She led them through the foyer and into an area marked as private.

Away from the public spaces, the decoration was more subdued. They passed along several corridors until the space opened up and they were suddenly by the stage of a London theatre.

Zaf gazed up, his jaw dropping open. The house

lights were up, and thirty or more people sat or stood. A dozen more people were on the stage itself. Scenery had been pushed back and the backdrop curtain had been lifted to create even more space. Drinks and nibbles were arranged on several tables.

"Backstage at a theatre," he whispered. "Like we've got access all areas passes or something."

"The excitement fades after a while," said the PA, Brie.

Brie put the two goody bags, hers and Serena's, on the floor beneath a table, just as Charlotte Webber took a glass from an attendant and tapped it with her fingernails to draw attention.

"Afternoon, everyone!" she said, projecting her voice into the auditorium. "I'm delighted to welcome Serena McNash of the Kenosha Falls Organisation and her team on their fact-finding mission in London."

There was scattered applause from the staff on the seats.

"Six years ago, my good friend and director Todd Granger introduced me to a very presumptuous songwriter by the name of Noah Dart" – there was knowing laughter from the audience and a whoop from somewhere – "who had the crazy notion of turning an obscure nineteenth-century poem about the industrialisation of the East End into a West End musical. I thought it was madness then and, six years later, I still think it's madness, but here we are."

More applause.

"We're here to help our American guests learn all they can, so they can make the planned transition of the play from this modest theatre to the heart of New York as straightforward as possible. Leave no question unanswered, leave no aspect unexplored." She raised her hands. "Eat, drink and be merry. But not too merry; we have a performance tonight."

Final applause morphed into a shuffle towards the food and booze.

Just ahead of Zaf, Serena drifted over to Charlotte.

"Thank you for your welcome," she said, then looked around. "No entertainment suite?"

"It's this, the tiny crew room, or the ghastly public bar," Charlotte told her. "The constraints of a theatre built in 1884. It's the same for most London theatres."

"It must be a nightmare," said Serena.

Charlotte shrugged. "It breeds a certain kind of discipline and plenty of creativity. We like to think we achieve amazing things. We're a pocket rocket of a theatre."

"Pocket rocket! That's adorable!"

Brie handed Serena a plate. "I chose the snacks that work for you. I checked the ingredients on everything."

"Did you touch these?" Serena asked.

"No, I used serving tongs."

Serena poked at the food on her plate then put it down on a side table. "All wrong." She went to the buffet table and picked out several of the miniature snacks.

Zaf drew closer to Brie. "The plate of food she's just assembled is a carbon copy of the one you gave her. What's that about?"

Brie's smile faltered. "She's the boss, what can I say? She gets a bit prickly, whatever I do." She shrugged.

"I'm sorry you're not appreciated." He looked over to the plates of tiny snacks. "What's good to eat on there? I feel like I need a magnifying glass."

Brie turned to him. "They're classic British dishes done as finger food. There's a fish goujon with a single chip, and a sausage slice with a dab of mash. There's even a really small toad in the hole that looks like a fairy cake."

"That sounds both amazing and a bit horrible too." Zaf wrinkled his nose. "You know toad in the hole?"

"I do."

"You're not American, are you?"

The young woman made a see-saw motion with her hand. "Canadian mum, British dad. I'm a foreigner everywhere I go. Honestly, the theatre is my home country." She laughed. "God, that sounded cheesy. But both my parents worked in theatre, and I suspect that out there" – she gestured to the auditorium seating – "I've got a couple of 'uncles' I really must say hello to."

She turned at the sound of movement under the

table. One of the gift bags violently tipped over and a small shape whipped away.

"What the...?" said Zaf.

Brie raised an eyebrow. "I'd say a certain cat is ransacking goody bags for rats in little red hats."

"Oh, Gus!" he hissed.

"*Gus: The Theatre Cat*," Brie said. "T.S. Eliot poem. From *Cats*."

"Really?"

"It's like destiny." She grinned.

Zaf left the stage, in pursuit of Gus and whatever toy bear he had in his jaws.

"He's not a theatre cat, Brie," he muttered. "He's a flipping nuisance."

Chapter Five

Zaf might have lived in London for a while, but a person who couldn't afford their own place to live certainly couldn't afford West End theatre tickets. He'd assumed that the theatres would be large, but he was wrong. This place was modest at best and had less than half the capacity of the Hippodrome in his home city of Birmingham.

Down at the front, three men leaned on the wall separating the front seats from the orchestra pit, holding drinks.

"Have you seen a cat come through here?" Zaf asked.

"See?" A balding man in a blue knitted jumper waved a long fruity cocktail carelessly. "That's the kind of small-talk icebreaker I'd never think of. 'Have you seen my cat?' Boom."

"Sorry, mate," slurred a man with bouncing curls. "No cats here, hep or otherwise."

"We're not supposed to be down here," said a quieter man with sallow skin. "Listening to Todd go on about old video files or whatever. We're supposed to be schmoozing."

"Noah, you couldn't schmooze if your life depended on it," said the curly-haired slurrer.

Zaf recognised the man from somewhere. He grinned as it came to him. "You're him off that thing."

The man held up his hands: *guilty as charged.* "Gareth Booncastle, for my sins. I was in a TV detective series called *Snoop!* Is that what you're thinking of?"

Zaf frowned: only old people watched TV. He'd recognised the man from YouTube videos about the show. "Great show. I'm amazed I didn't recognise you earlier."

"It's my superpower," Gareth told him. "I get recognised thanks to my hair. If I pop a hat on then I'm just a regular bloke. It works in reverse, like how my stunt double becomes me when he puts on the wig." He looked around at his companions, raising an eyebrow. "I'm actually a hollow shell. Every single aspect of me is a studied persona, even Gareth."

"So you're all part of this?" Zaf waved a hand to indicate the theatre.

Gareth grunted. "Lead actor is what I am. Jack Ha'penny, 'umble Cockney costermonger and pavement artist, at your service. Noah here's our creative."

"The songwriter." Zaf nodded. "Great tunes. That one Adele covered, I liked that."

"He wrote the songs and the music," said Gareth. "He's a genius at all that, but he's not a natural schmoozer, are you, sweets?"

Noah rolled his eyes. "You're really helping, Gareth. Build me up, why don't you?"

Gareth ignored him and pointed to the balding cocktail drinker. "Todd here is the UK director. He *does* know how to schmooze, but he'd rather avoid it and talk shop instead. Hangover, Todd?"

"Not at all," said Todd. "I'm letting them soak in the place while I take a breather. I'd rather hide in my office, to be frank."

This drew chuckles from the other two.

Gareth turned to Zaf. "Our poor director doesn't have an office. It's a sore point, particularly since he's been working non-stop on this thing. The deal, I mean."

"So, is the show going to America then?" said Zaf. "Or is that...?"

Todd barked with laughter, his movements blurry. "Theatre. It's all illusion. Smoke and mirrors." He leaned towards Zaf. "And the business is doubly so. Is the contract signed? Do we still need to suck up to the Yanks, or can we relax? All is in flux."

He stopped himself, his back stiffening.

Zaf looked round to see Serena descending from the stage, Brie in tow.

"Serena." Todd tugged at the collar of his jumper, the cocktail glass jiggling in his other hand. "Lovely to meet you at last. Todd Granger."

He held out a hand which she shook politely.

"My trifecta of talent," she said. "The director, the writer and the actor." She gave Gareth an admiring look. "I intend to pack the famous Snoop in my suitcase when I head home."

Zaf looked between the British trio. Gareth was looking sniffy, while the other two watched him.

"I *have* had other roles," Gareth said. "I received an Olivier, Evening Standard Award and Critic's Circle Award for my dual role of Jonathan Harker and Dracula at the Royal National Theatre."

"What a clever boy you are," Serena replied. "But I do hope you're not one of those temperamental artiste types."

"I can be whatever type of artiste is required, darling. My range is legendary. People get hung up on the success of *Snoop!*" He raised his chin. "But the truth is, I'm very versatile."

"Versatile enough to bring life to *The Cockney's Complaint* in Broadway, at least."

Irritation flickered briefly across Gareth's face before he gave her a broad smile. "Oh, I can't wait. I've been to New York many times, of course, but an extended stay in the Big Apple? It will be an absolute tonic, I can tell you!"

He tossed his beautifully unruly hair.

"Well that's great news," said Serena, a hand resting on his arm. She looked at Noah Dart. "And do you have any fresh musical gold in that cranium of yours that you'd consider bringing directly to me?"

"Always writing something," Noah replied. "Which reminds me. I must have a word with the technical crew about the sound for tonight's show. Excuse me." He gave them a nod and retreated.

Gareth took a step towards Serena. "I did wonder if we could have a quick private word about my contract. There're a few clauses I'd like to discuss."

Serena gave him a playful look and offered him her arm. "You can talk about it all you like."

As they moved off, Todd and Brie exchanged awkward glances. Zaf watched them, curious.

At last, both Todd and Brie spluttered with laughter.

"Well, are we going to stand on ceremony?" Todd said.

Brie wrapped her arms around him. Todd responded with a bear hug that lifted her off her feet. He put her down and held her back to get a good look at her.

"You were..." He saw Zaf, standing there, watching. "Last time I saw this one, she was knee high to a grasshopper."

Brie was red-faced and laughing. "This is one of those uncles I mentioned."

"Big friend of her dad's," Todd said, his eyes not leaving her face.

"Penniless artistes together."

"Oh, you make it sound like we lived on absinthe and cigarettes." Todd gave Zaf a glance. "Our repertory theatre days."

"Penniless artistes," Brie repeated.

"I brought you a gift." Todd looked about himself as though it should have been there. "Later. Tell me everything. How is your old mum? Still with the sun-worshipping cult in Los Angeles?"

"It's Santa Barbara and it's an organic farming commune," she said, "but yes."

Zaf cleared his throat. "That sounds lovely. But I need to go and find my cat." He sidled away.

He moved down the front row, towards a woman in a black stage crew outfit.

"You're not looking for a cat, are you?" she asked.

He felt relief wash over him. "Yes."

She pointed towards a small, featureless door out of the auditorium, right next to the stage.

He smiled at her. "Thanks." He headed off, his relief dimming as he realised he had no idea where he was going.

He passed through the door and along a corridor. It was functionally decorated with exposed brickwork and electrical wiring hooked to the side walls.

Through an open door he saw racks of clothes, and found himself drawn by the explosion of colours and materials.

No, he told himself. *Don't be tempted.* He had to find Gus.

A shadow moved by an open fire exit door. He went through it.

"Oh Gus, you'd better not have wandered outside."

He stepped out into a narrow alley running along the side of the theatre.

"Gus?"

The alley was empty.

Zaf turned back and approached the door to go back inside.

"I'm sorry, you can't come in here."

An older man stood in the doorway. He wore a doorman's uniform and had the brick-wall presence of a nightclub bouncer. But he was more distinguished than any bouncer Zaf had encountered.

"You don't understand. I was inside there and I just came out to find my cat." Zaf pointed along the alleyway.

The man ran a hand over his shiny bald head. "There's no cats in the Delphinium Theatre." His accent was London with a hint of Nigeria. "I suggest you go round to the front and buy a ticket."

Zaf looked at the man, his chest tight. This sort of thing happened to him all the time. He was a young black man, and on top of that he had what his mum called an 'impish' look.

He peered at the name badge on the man's lapel. "Farrell. You've got to believe me, mate. I was just in there."

Farrell the doorman was unmoved. "D'you have any idea how many people come round here and try to talk their way backstage?" He shook his head. "You need to go round the front and speak to the box office."

"But didn't you just see me come out of this door a minute ago?"

Farrell folded his arms across his chest. "Sorry, mate."

Zaf gave up. It would be quicker to go back in through the foyer.

As he turned to trudge back along the alley, a blur of grey shot past him and in through the open door.

"Gus!"

Farrell gave no indication that he had seen the cat.

"Didn't you just see the cat?" Zaf asked.

Farrell ignored him, turning to another man approaching the door. "Evening, sir."

Farrell tipped his hat and stepped aside for the new arrival to go inside.

Zaf swore under his breath and made his way towards the main entrance.

Chapter Six

On the stage, by the buffet, Diana looked at Reuben. She was determined not to give up.

"See that silver platter?" she said. "That's Italy, right? Now the smaller platters around it are parts of the Roman Empire, about two thousand years ago. Romans would have been in all of these places, building Roman things. Two thousand years ago."

"Right." Reuben pursed his lips.

Diana held up a finger. "Now, if we take this tiny dish of olives and put it over here on a separate table, this is modern Rome. So two thousand years later, the number of Romans, these olives, is much smaller. And they're not building historic monuments in the name of Rome anymore. So we don't really notice them so much."

Reuben studied the table. He moved a couple of olives. "The Romans who lived in London before would have had families, so there should still be Romans here. I just need to find them."

Diana thought of the two thousand years of genetics and history separating Roman Britons from any descendants they might have today.

She'd never convince Reuben.

"Surely you can use DNA to find people in London with Roman ancestry," said Charlotte Webber, approaching them. "There are probably loads of them."

The theatre manager shook Reuben's hand. "Good to put a face to the man juggling our numbers and counting our pennies." She gave Diana a sly side look. "He's been kicking the tyres and questioning our efficiency."

"*The Cockney's Complaint* seems very successful," said Diana.

"You have to offset that against the costs of putting on a production," Charlotte said.

"Costs beyond your wildest imaginings," said Reuben. "Transferring a show to Broadway can be a financial nightmare."

"And a practical one," Charlotte added.

"But an exciting move?" suggested Diana.

Charlotte gave her a brittle smile. "It's exciting for lots of people. For me, the deal means we'll lose our core production team here at the Delphinium."

"Oh?" Diana hadn't expected that. "Will you need a new cast and crew?"

Charlotte nodded. "A new director and a new Jack Ha'penny. They're not jobs many people can do."

"Can't you find another TV actor?" asked Reuben.

"Don't let Mr Booncastle hear you call him a TV actor or he'll be droning on about his two Oliviers until we all fall asleep," Charlotte said. "He's a big draw, though. Todd Granger will be harder to replace."

"The director," Diana said.

"It's Todd that brought the entire vision to life. It might be Noah's songs, but someone needs to tie the artistic bow around it all." Charlotte sighed. "If I had my way, he'd stay with the Delphinium forever."

"High praise."

Reuben had turned towards the food table. Diana was about to do the same when she heard a creak from above.

She turned, puzzled. Something had caught her eye, a shift in the light shining down on the stage.

She looked up and gasped.

Something was falling: a shape, Diana couldn't make out what.

Without thinking, she threw out her brolly to hold Reuben Romano back.

She blinked, realising the falling shape was a man.

It – he – crashed down through the buffet table with a bone-crunching snap. Food catapulted in all directions.

There were shouts and a few screams. Within the wreckage of the crushed table, the man's limbs were twisted at awkward angles.

"What?" whispered Reuben in shock, just inches away from the fallen man.

Diana stepped forward, crouching to apply first aid.

Too late.

The balding man was dead, his empty gaze fixed on a point high above.

Charlotte looked down at the man, then let out a gasp.

"Oh my God. It's Todd."

Chapter Seven

Zaf strode along the alleyway and back to the front of the theatre, steaming with indignation. The woman Diana had winked at as they'd come in was still at the box office desk. She was on the phone to someone, her expression grave.

"Yes, the Delphinium. Coventry Street. I don't know the details. Seriously injured, I think."

Zaf stopped in front of her and pointed at himself, then at the doors, hoping she'd remember him coming in earlier. She frowned and waved him on, pre-occupied.

He gave her a thumbs-up. She ignored him, intent on her phone call.

The doors into the theatre auditorium were locked but there was another door to the side which Zaf hoped would take him in the right direction. He went through and up the stairs, expecting to come out in the upper circle or somewhere.

A minute later he realised he was wrong. A switch-back maze of corridors had brought him up to another corridor that ran along the length of the theatre. Through an open door, he saw a dimly lit room dominated by screens and sound mixing boards. One screen was paused on an image, a washed-out old video showing a small girl in a yellow princess dress and a plastic tiara frozen mid-dance, framed against a glass door. But the room – a light and sound booth? – was empty.

A long window looked out from the room, over the auditorium and stage. He approached it and realised how high up he was.

"Oh, this is cool."

He scanned the theatre auditorium below, hoping for a vantage point from which he could locate Gus. Then he froze.

He pulled closer to the window, hand on the glass, trying to work out what had happened down there.

It didn't look good.

Debris and scattered tablecloths littered the stage and a small group of people, one with a bulky green first aid box, were gathered around something. Everyone else was down by the seats, huddled in shock.

Zaf squinted, looking for Diana.

She was onstage, with the group of people.

Someone moved, and now Zaf could see what it was they were standing around.

It was a man.

Zaf felt his stomach lurch as he saw the twisted shape the man lay in.

Look away.

A few feet away from Diana stood the American production accountant, Reuben. He had a plate in his hand and was placing buffet morsels into his mouth, his expression neutral.

Zaf stepped back. His hand brushed a drinking glass: long and curved, with a fruity residue smearing its inner surface. It seemed out of place up here.

"What the hell are you doing here?"

Zaf turned. He blinked.

In the doorway stood Noah Dart, the songwriter. His expression wavered between tense and distraught. Behind him was a member of the theatre crew.

"I was just..." Zaf shrugged, glancing back over the auditorium.

"Get out of here! Downstairs."

Zaf nodded. He left the room. How would he get down to the stage? He had to know what had happened. He had to help.

As he left the room, Noah pushed past him with the woman from the crew.

"What did Todd say?" Zaf heard Noah snap.

"He wanted to review some video files for the

Americans. He seemed" – the woman hesitated – "odd."

"Odd?"

Zaf, in the corridor, paused.

"He said his hands felt numb," the woman said.

"Numb?"

"Yes. Numb."

"He did have heart problems."

"He was agitated. Out of sorts."

"Did he say he was going to check the lighting rigs?" asked Noah.

"Why would the director go and check lighting rigs?"

"I don't know! Where's the production electrician, um...?"

"Christos."

"Christos. Go get him."

"But—"

"Now! I want to know what happened."

Zah heard the woman moving back to the door. He made off along the corridor.

Down in the lobby, the doors to the theatre had been flung wide. An ambulance was parked on the pavement right outside, its lights throwing distorted shapes against the walls.

The chaos he'd seen in the theatre had expanded out into the foyer. People spread out in knots of quiet, stunned confusion.

Zaf entered the theatre. Diana was onstage, talking to a paramedic.

His phone buzzed: a message from Newton Crombie.

Have you seen Gus anywhere?

I'm not sure, thought Zaf. And besides, now wasn't the time.

Chapter Eight

When the traffic had let him through and the authorities had finally granted access, Newton brought the bus to the theatre to take the visitors back to their hotel. His surprise at the death onstage was eclipsed by his worry about Gus's whereabouts.

"I need to go and look," he kept muttering.

"You can't," Diana told him. "There are more important things to deal with."

He gave her a perplexed look. "But Gus..."

She shook her head. "Not now."

Diana pushed back her panic and concern and pulled on a smile as she ushered the Americans back onto the bus. They were preoccupied, a number of them absorbed with their phones as they drove back to the hotel. Brie barely even heard when Penny told her that a package had been sent up to her room. Diana watched as the group stumbled through the foyer of the Redhouse Hotel, making for their rooms and a moment of calm.

Once the bus had been put to bed, as Newton put it, Zaf and Diana set off home together. Normally they walked separately; being housemates and colleagues was enough. But today, she needed company, and it seemed he did too.

"Do many people die in the theatre?" Zaf asked as they crossed Oxford Street.

Diana dodged a group of women holding Selfridges bags. "A lot can go wrong in theatres. Equipment, ropes."

Zaf stepped to one side, narrowly avoiding being swiped by an open bag with something that looked a lot like a Paddington toy poking out of it. "I heard someone say the man had a heart condition."

She nodded as they started walking along Park Lane, leaving the worst of the crowds behind. "Bernard Bresslaw, Leonard Rossiter and Tommy Cooper all died of heart attacks in London theatres. Tommy Cooper died right on stage, and at first everyone thought it was part of his act."

Zaf's face was blank: he had no idea who she was talking about.

"Heart condition or not," she continued, "it was a

strange decision for a director to climb the lighting rig during a drinks reception."

"Why would he do that?"

She shook her head. "They'll have to find another director for the American show."

"He was due to go over?" Zaf asked.

"Todd and that floppy-haired actor, Gareth Boon-castle, were planning to set up the show in the States. I don't think Charlotte was happy to see her talent fleeing the Delphinium."

Zaf nodded. The two of them carried on walking, passing Hyde Park on their right and Mayfair on the left. They approached Hyde Park Corner and the Wellington Arch.

"It'll ruin the rest of the tour," said Zaf.

Diana sighed. "We'll have to do our best to prevent that."

Zaf straightened up as they walked under the underpass towards Grosvenor Place. "So, about the vanilla and almond body crème you've been putting on your hands..."

"Yes?"

"If I were to go home now and get in the shower, would there be any other stuff missing?"

She looked at him, amused at his attempt to be tactful.

"Definitely," she replied. "Some of your products smell very nice."

Zaf frowned. "There are some specialised products there."

"Little jars and pots. I noticed. A lot of them."

"That healing clay is only to be used in tiny amounts, on bites or shaving rash."

She went over the contents of the bathroom in her mind's eye. "Is that the paste that smells of menthol?"

"Yes."

"It's nice and stimulating on my neck. I love it."

He stopped walking. "It's sixty quid a pot!"

"That's ridiculous. Who'd pay that kind of money?"

Zaf's face was reddening. "Seriously, it's not for slapping on in the shower. Same as the conditioning oil, which is for beards. One or two drops a week, and that's been disappearing, too."

"Oh, the patchouli stuff? The smell's like being back in the eighties. It works wonders on taming my hair if I comb it through on the final rinse."

"Final rinse? You're joking me? That stuff is a hundred and twenty a bottle."

She scoffed. "Well, they clearly saw you coming."

Zaf carried on walking. "Connie got it me for Christmas as a special treat."

"Your sister? Saw her coming too, then."

Diana did feel bad about using Zaf's products. Especially since she had no idea how he afforded prices like that. But after today, an argument would do them good. And she was getting tired of his clutter.

"Maybe if you didn't leave them lying around then I wouldn't be tempted to use them," she said.

"They're not *lying around*. They're organised."

"Oh. Well, I'm sorry. But while we're on the subject of things being used, I noticed we're out of orange juice again."

He raised an eyebrow. "You said I could have some."

"I did. But I bought that new carton yesterday and now it's empty."

"I had some."

Diana pressed her lips together. "*Some*. The whole box. Am I going to have to start hiding it, like the biscuits?"

He clenched a fist. "I *knew* you were doing that!"

"You looked for them. I can tell."

"Why don't you write *biscuit experiment* on the packet. You seem to think it works if you put *milk experiment* on the milk."

Diana suppressed a laugh. The labels *had* worked.

They were nearing home. Had she cleared the air? Or had she made things worse?

Zaf was young. She had no idea if he'd ever house-shared before.

"I'm sorry about your products," she said as they walked past Victoria Station. Commuters were pouring out of its exits, buses queueing up for the bus stops.

"Yeah." He didn't make eye contact.

She sighed. The argument hadn't made her feel better.

"I think I might go and potter around the square for half an hour," she said.

"Yeah, sure." He turned away from her towards the flat.

Chapter Nine

Diana rented a huge flat on the middle floor of a house in Eccleston Square, Pimlico. Zaf still couldn't believe how grand it was, how big the garden in the centre of the square was. A garden just for the lucky so-and-sos who lived there.

He'd never live in a place like this, not properly. Diana only did because of her weird rent arrangement. He let himself in and climbed the wide staircase to the first floor.

He chucked his keys into the bowl by the door, still fuming at the cost of the things she'd been using so casually. Like he could afford to throw that stuff around!

But he knew how much he was saving on rent, living here. And a part of him felt guilty for having a go at her.

The guilt was worse. It reminded him he was trapped: unable to get a place of his own.

Huffing, he pulled off his work shirt and threw it onto the chair in his bedroom. It fell to the floor. He went to pick it up, then paused to look at the chair. It was old, the seat made from woven cane. It was practical and also very lovely.

Everything in Diana's flat was like that. There was nothing from Ikea or a catalogue. This was a house furnished not only with love but with the accumulated possessions of a life well lived.

Recently, he'd been helping her clear out the flat on the top floor of the house. Bryan McGivern, who'd lived here as long as Diana, had died, and they'd been doing their best to find new homes for his possessions.

Every piece of furniture in Bryan's flat, every wall hanging, every throw, every odd-shaped pot in the kitchen, came with a story. Zaf knew that made it difficult for Diana to clear it all out. And her flat was no different. This place he'd been invited to share wasn't just accommodation. It was her home and her life.

"Damn it."

He'd been too harsh.

He pulled his shirt back on and went downstairs to find her.

On the ground floor, the landlord Alexsei Dadashov was by the door, sorting the post. Alexsei lived in the ground floor flat from time to time, though

Zaf reckoned he – or at least his super-rich dad – had other properties across the city.

"Hi, Alexsei."

Alexsei gazed at him. The young man had dark eyes and heavy eyebrows which would have been cute if they weren't so disconcerting when he stared like that.

"You are still here," he said.

"I am. Diana's still kind enough to be putting me up."

"She is," said Alexsei. "Too kind, perhaps."

"I'm hoping it's only temporary."

"I like Diana."

"I like her too."

Alexsei seemed unconvinced. "I would not be happy if I saw someone take advantage of her kindness."

Zaf smiled, trying to convince Alexsei he wasn't like that. He knew he was failing. The smile probably made him look even more shifty.

He took a deep breath. "I'm a good person, though."

Had he really just said that?

Alexsei raised an eyebrow and went back to the post.

Rattled, Zaf trudged back upstairs. He shook himself out and went to the wide living room window overlooking the square.

Diana was outside one of the other houses, tidying

a window box. Diana liked to tend the empty houses, trimming unruly plants and sometimes planting new ones.

A woman walking along with a yoga mat under her arm stopped to chat to her. Zaf watched them, the ease of their body language.

He wanted to dash down and apologise, maybe offer to help her. But the moment had passed. Todd Granger's death had set his nerves on edge. Not to mention the way Alexsei had just spoken to him.

He emptied the contents of his backpack and went to get a shower.

He'd tidy up, move all the products back into his room. It meant his stuff wouldn't get used. It also meant the place would be less cluttered.

Chapter Ten

Diana woke after a troubled night's sleep. She stood under the shower, then hesitated as her hand reached for shampoo and soap. She opened her eyes, remembering to grab her own.

Zaf's bedroom door was still closed; that wasn't unusual. She headed downstairs and began her walk to work. Other than on the very dreariest days, the walk was her favourite way to start the day. Zaf, on the other hand, preferred to catch the number 13 bus from Victoria.

She arrived early at the Chartwell and Crouch bus depot in Chiltern Street, and noticed posters up around the place that hadn't been there yesterday. The depot manager, Paul Kensington, must have been in. Every single poster was advertising his ridiculous "Londiniumarium".

The Londiniumarium was supposed to deliver what Paul called 'the London experience' in a single location, taking the touring out of tourism. A warehouse had been fitted out with all sorts of nonsense so tourists didn't need to travel around the capital. Why bother physically visiting the sights when a version of those sights could be brought to you?

Diana had been hoping the whole thing would die a swift death, her hopes resting on the twin pillars of the stupidity of the idea and Paul's notorious ineptitude, a characteristic that meant he rarely saw anything through.

"Bugger," she said with feeling.

She read through the poster and her heart sank even further. Today was the launch day.

She hurried into the kitchen to pick up the day's itinerary. A pink post-it note had been attached to the paper.

Diana,

All of today's activities are scrubbed. You'll spend the day treating your guests to a VIP experience at the Londiniumarium. They will be the first guests through the doors. Make sure they know how lucky they are!

Paul

Diana sank into a chair and groaned.

After a few moments, she stirred. The only thing she could do was what she always did in a crisis.

She put the kettle on.

Newton Crombie arrived just after it had boiled. "Have you found him?" he asked.

Diana turned to him. "Who?"

"Gus."

She stared at him. "I hadn't been looking to be honest, Newton. A lot happened yesterday."

He shook his head. "I was wandering around Leicester Square and Chinatown until late last night, shaking a bag of his favourite DreamTreats."

Diana raised an eyebrow. "Get any takers?"

Newton's gaze dropped to the floor. "I made friends with a few local cats."

Diana felt worry prickle at her, remembering what had happened a few weeks ago when Gus had first taken up residence.

"You didn't bring any of them back here, did you?" she said. "You have a reputation."

"I did not." Newton's tone was clipped. "Gus is my cat now."

Diana nodded. "Don't forget he was a street cat before he made this place his home. He'll be fine. He's probably having the time of his life exploring the theatre."

Newton didn't seem convinced.

He spotted a pile of spare posters scattered on the table. "What's this?" He picked one up. "Londinium-ah, Londinium-ay, how do you even say it?" He searched in the dishwasher for his favourite mug while he attempted to pronounce the word, mumbling under his breath. "I'm pretty sure a word like that'll summon a demon."

"Apparently we're going there today," Diana said.

Newton sagged into a chair opposite her. "And these poor people are the guinea pigs?"

"Who's a guinea pig?" asked Zaf as he entered. Diana turned to him just as he spotted the posters. "Oh, this is going to be bad."

"But it's what we're doing, apparently," said Diana, "so we'll just have to make it the best possible version of awful that we can."

Zaf sighed and Newton went back to his muttering. Diana sipped her tea, unconvinced by her own forced optimism.

After they'd all drunk their tea and done their best to psych themselves up for the horrors of the day, they drove to the hotel. As Newton parked the bus, Diana turned to Zaf.

"You look miserable."

He shrugged.

"You can't look like that for the guests. We need to pretend."

He pulled on a rictus smile, staring into her face. She sighed and stood back to let him onto the bus.

He paused, looking at the woman standing outside the hotel. "What's going on?"

Diana looked over his shoulder. Just outside the doors to the Redhouse Hotel stood a police officer in a yellow hi-vis jacket and peaked cap. She was ignoring them, speaking into a radio.

"I take it you've seen a policewoman before," Diana said to Zaf.

"I have a bad feeling about this," he muttered.

Chapter Eleven

The American visitors had already gathered in the hotel lobby. They sat quietly, many scrolling through their phones. No one looked in the mood for a trip out.

Zaf went to reception, leaving Diana with the group.

"Morning, Penny," he said. "Have they been this quiet since they got back yesterday?"

Penny Slipper nodded. "Their trip got off to a rocky start. How are you all holding up?"

He pulled a face. "Not great."

Diana had started chatting to the guests, and a couple were even on their feet.

"At least they look like they're planning to go out with you," Penny said. "I was worried they'd mope around here all day."

He gave her a wink. "As if they'd have time to mope when they're on a Chartwell and Crouch tour."

"Someone else might have plans for them." Penny jerked her head to the side.

Zaf turned to see three people approaching: Charlotte Webber and Noah Dart, accompanied by a man instantly recognisable as a police detective.

Detective Chief Inspector Clint Sugarbrook was almost as wide as he was tall, twenty-stone of wrestler physique dressed up in a suit and tie and, the ultimate cliché, a tan-coloured trench coat.

"What's he doing here?" Zaf whispered.

"They think the director's death was suspicious," replied Penny.

"They do?"

"I heard something about cocaine in his bloodstream. Vast quantities, apparently."

Zaf's eyes widened.

Sugarbrook, Charlotte and Noah stopped in front of the group.

"Everyone," said Charlotte. "It's been a difficult twenty-four hours for us all. Todd's death has... it's punched a huge hole in both our personal and our professional lives. I've spoken to his ex-wife and children in Edinburgh and informed them of the situation."

There were solemn nods. Zaf spotted red rings around Brie's eyes.

"Though the personal tragedy dominates," Charlotte continued, "the cancellation of last night's performance has only heightened emotions around the production. To top it all, the police have questions for us regarding the incident." She licked her lips. "Personally, I feel a day out seeing the sights might be best for all of us, but Clint Sugarbrook here—"

"Detective Chief Inspector," interrupted the detective.

"—would like to ask you some questions."

"Formal questions?" asked Diana.

Sugarbrook looked at Diana. He frowned, then his gaze snagged on her duck's head umbrella. His eyes narrowed.

"Miss... Bakewell," he said.

"I was just wondering if you might like to accompany us for the day," Diana said. "A bit of a bus ride. A chance to chat to people."

"I'm not sure..."

"You could get your colleague outside to collect you when you're done."

Sugarbrook grunted. He looked around the group, then shrugged.

Diana smiled at him, but he only scowled back. She'd convinced him, but he wasn't happy about it.

"That's settled then," said Diana. "Everyone, let's get onto the bus."

As they stepped onto the pavement, Zaf noticed the actor, Gareth Booncastle, speaking to Newton through the open front door.

"If I *do* see your cat when I'm onstage tonight, I shall be certain to let you know immediately."

He turned to face the approaching tour group with a grin that was too wide and much too cheery.

"Here we all are!" Gareth boomed. "Thought I'd surprise you by joining you all on your little tour. Eh, Serena? Fun surprise, huh?"

"Delightful," said the American.

Zaf heard Charlotte and Noah exchange tuts.

"Come to try to bump up his pay cheque?" whispered Noah.

"Oh, didn't you hear about the Spielberg thing?" Charlotte whispered back.

"Spielberg?"

"Our big-haired ham's star is in the ascendant, Noah. Watch this space."

As they all got on the bus, Brie was chatting to the accountant, Reuben. She beckoned Zaf towards them.

"Mr Romano wanted to know if the water here is safe to drink," she said. "I tried to assure him."

In his short time in this job, Zaf had learned not to be surprised at people's questions.

"You can drink the tap water," he said. "It's perfectly safe."

"Like *safe* safe?" asked Reuben. "I've been using the water from the minibar for brushing my teeth."

"It's safe, sir," Zaf replied. "The safest."

Diana picked up the microphone as the bus pulled away. "Today you have the privilege of being VIP guests at a brand-new facility. But we'll begin with a brief drive along Baker Street. Has anyone here heard of Sherlock Holmes?"

Almost everyone's hands shot up, and Zaf smiled. Americans were so much better at audience participation than Brits.

"You all work in the arts in some form or another," Diana said, "so I'm sure I don't need to add my usual reminder that he was and is a fictional character."

The police detective had taken one of the rear seats and was talking to Noah Dart. Zaf was a few seats in front of them and could hear their conversation: Sugarbrook was making no effort to lower his voice.

"I don't know what habits you might be referring to," Noah said.

"Mr Granger is dead," said Sugarbrook. "So there's no reason to protect him. All I'm asking is if you were aware of him having a drug habit."

"Not that I *saw*," said Noah.

Reuben turned in his seat to face Sugarbrook. "Is it really true what they say about British bobbies?"

"That they keep their sandwiches under their tall helmets?" suggested Sugarbrook.

"That none of them are packing?"

"Packing? Oh, firearms. Yes, that's true. The UK has the largest unarmed police force in the world."

"Sheesh." Reuben shook his head.

"We tend to find," said Sugarbrook, "that people are less likely to get hurt if there are no guns involved."

"Fine and dandy until some lunatic starts going round killing people."

"We have few killers here. London is a surprisingly safe city."

"Jack the Ripper!" said Reuben.

"Well, yes. But he's been fairly quiet for a few years—"

"The last murder was in 1891," called Diana from the front.

Sugarbrook pursed his lips. "So we probably don't need to worry about him."

Reuben didn't seem satisfied. "You never know."

"We don't?"

"Could be a killer lurking round the very next corner."

"Let's hope not, eh?" said Sugarbrook.

Chapter Twelve

Zaf joined Diana near the front. There was a selection of Londiniumarium flyers in the plastic rack by the front seats. He glanced through one.

"It looks a bit rubbish."

"But we're going to make it fun," said Diana.

"I mean, what even is a holographic River Thames?"

Diana shrugged. "Paul said something about an audio-visual experience with smells pumped into the room."

Zaf gestured towards the window. "But the River Thames is right there." He looked out. "Well, it's there somewhere. Not hard to find."

"I know. Look, I don't think this is a good idea either. But Paul's the boss and he says we have to go there. I wish we could have seen it beforehand instead of doing this without any preparation, but that's just what we'll have to do."

Zaf read through the rest of the flyer as they drove along the inner ring road towards Shoreditch. It wasn't until they were about halfway there that he was struck by a thought. "All of these things at the Londiniumnium."

"Londiniumarium," said Diana.

"Londiginarium."

"Londiniumarium."

"Lond-diddle-diddle-arium. Whatever. This place just sounds like rooms our customers will walk through. What's our role in all this?"

Diana sighed. "And there, in a nutshell, is the problem with Paul Kensington. So keen to cut costs and impress head office, that he'll undermine what Chartwell and Crouch is built upon. I think he sees a future where personal tour guides are not needed. A conveyor belt of buses dropping off tourists to be shoved through his tourism sausage machine."

Zaf grimaced. Treating people like pieces of meat for the smallest amount of money was definitely the Paul Kensington way.

Newton pulled up into a car park behind a warehouse building which bore faint outlines of a sign from years gone by.

Gordon Hamlet & Sons, Cabinetmakers

A ghost sign: now he knew what they were, Zaf

had spotted them all over London. The newer, brighter sign declared that they were in '*The Londiniumarium — all of London under one roof.*'

Diana handed him the microphone and he stood up.

"Welcome everyone! Welcome to the Londinium — er — arium."

He breathed a sigh of relief. Reading it out slowly was the only way he could make it all the way through such a stupid word.

"The what?" called one of the Americans.

Zaf ignored the question. "We'll make our way to reception and get your VIP passes, shall we?"

Brie and Noah Dart walked side by side across the car park.

"I barely got any time to talk to him," Zaf heard Brie say. "I hadn't seen Todd in a lifetime. One hug, a moment's reunion, and then he was dead."

Noah nodded sadly. He reached up a hand to her shoulder then shook his head just slightly and dropped it to his side.

"If my friendship with your dad taught me any-thing," Noah said, "it's that we never get as much time with our loved ones as we'd like."

"You knew Brie's dad?" Zaf said.

Noah looked at him. "Mitch. Mitch Grebbson. An-other musician."

"My dad was welded to his piano," Brie said. "Half my memories are of him sitting there, tripping out ditties. The man, the piano. I'm not sure I remember him having legs."

"Music was fun for him," Noah nodded. "He didn't care that he was so gifted." He sighed. "Not a soulless sell-out like me."

The group went inside. The reception was decorated with bright lights and solid plastic panelling. Neon lights were arranged into a union jack pattern on one wall.

Zaf stared at it all, apprehensive. It felt they were about to enter an ultra-patriotic bowling alley or soft play centre.

"Is this what passes for entertainment these days?" said DCI Sugarbrook.

A solitary man stood behind the reception desk, wearing a bow tie that he kept tugging at.

"Good morning!" he said. "My name is Raffles, gentleman at leisure, expert cricketer, and jewellery thief. I am here to welcome you all today."

Zaf rolled his eyes.

"Hello, Raffles," said Diana. "You're expecting a party from Chartwell and Crouch?"

"Yes! Your VIP passes are here. Please put them around your necks."

Raffles handed out the largest and most cumbersome lanyard passes Zaf had ever seen. If anyone wearing one happened to step into a gust of wind, they'd be swept away like an umbrella in a hurricane.

"Why are they so big?" asked Serena.

"Mr Kensington says to print everything in the largest possible sizes for our visually impaired visitors and colleagues," said Raffles.

Serena narrowed her eyes. "Where's yours then, Raffles?"

Raffles flushed. He clutched his hands to his chest, as if searching for the missing lanyard. "Ah, yes. Well, I told you my name, didn't I?"

"In that case, I am Serena and I will no longer be needing this." Serena thrust her lanyard at Brie.

As the group was waved through to the next room, Raffles barred Zaf's way.

"Excuse me, you're Zaf, yes?" he asked in a quiet yet urgent tone.

Zaf pointed at his outsized lanyard. "I've got mile-high letters around my neck saying so."

"Right. Yes. Mr Kensington said you might step in and help. We've had our Pearly King call in sick."

Zaf stared.

Diana cleared her throat. "What would Zaf need to do, exactly?"

Raffles gave her a nervous smile. "He pops on his clothes, he comes in when we play God Save the King, and then he does a cheery little dance with the Pearly Prime Minister. The steps are easy."

Zaf waved a hand at his face. "So, I'm like, King Charles? Like, the actual king?"

"That's right."

"I'm black. The king's white, last time I looked. People are gonna notice a detail like that."

"Ever heard of colour-blind casting?" replied Raffles. "Mr Kensington says you're the best choice."

From the wringing of Raffles' hands, Zaf suspected that he was the only choice.

He turned to Diana, his arms outstretched. "What do I do?"

"I don't know, Zaf. Think you can manage it?"

Zaf shrugged and threw his arms down to the sides.

"Come on Raffles, let's go find this outfit. At least I'm not one of the poor tour group, having to watch this thing." He shook his head. "First they have to endure the murder of a colleague, and now this..."

Chapter Thirteen

"Let's go through here and you can catch the Tube Experience to your next destination," said Raffles.

He led them down a corridor. Diana followed, wondering how vast the space was beyond the panelling on either side of them. At last they entered a room laid out like a London Underground carriage. They all shuffled in and sat on the moquette seating.

"This layout emulates the smaller carriages of the deeper underground lines," said Raffles, reading from an information plaque. "Whereas some of the sub-surface lines have larger carriages, with a wider space between the seats."

Sugarbrook caught Diana's eye. She shrugged.

"Everyone ready?" Raffles asked. "Hold tight."

He flicked a switch and the carriage began to

rumble and sway. There was a screeching noise that made Diana wince, and gasps from the tour group.

How long were they supposed to sit here? Raffles wasn't looking like he was about to switch the thing off any time soon.

Diana stared up at the maps and the adverts on the wall above the heads of her companions. Instead of advertising wellness vitamins and car insurance, the adverts were for the other attractions and the specials in the Londiniumarium cafeteria.

2 for the price of 1 on London Eye-screams Double choc-chip!

She grimaced.

Eventually Raffles flicked the switch and the swaying and screeching stopped.

Reuben looked even paler than usual. "I feel nauseous. Why did that go on for so long? In fact, why did we have to endure it at all?"

"Right you are, sir. Walk this way, sir, if you will."

Raffles led them through another door into a new area.

"Quite realistic, if you ask me," said Sugarbrook.

Gareth Booncastle fell into step with Sugarbrook behind Diana as they walked along the next corridor.

"I played a detective on television," said Gareth. "You've probably seen it."

Sugarbrook gave him the side-eye. "I don't watch police shows. My constant complaining detracts from my wife's enjoyment."

"I've always been proud of the way *Snoop!* stayed true to the spirit of genuine detective work."

"The mind-numbing tedium and paperwork?" replied Sugarbrook.

Gareth ignored the comment. "I take it this is just a courtesy visit. You don't really think Todd's death is suspicious?"

"Don't you?" replied Sugarbrook. "What was he doing up there in the lighting rigs when the rest of the group was downstairs?"

Gareth's voice dropped. "Didn't someone on the tech team say he'd been agitated? Not himself."

Sugarbrook said nothing.

"It was his heart, right?" continued Gareth.

"You knew he had a heart condition?"

"He was an out of shape man in his fifties."

"Had he been drinking that day?"

"A big colourful cocktail."

"What cocktail?"

"I didn't ask. Maybe it was just fruit juice."

"I see."

There was a door ahead. Diana followed the rest of the group towards it, still listening to Sugarbrook and Gareth.

"These are just unofficial questions, right?" said Gareth, his tone uneasy. "You're not going to go poking round the theatre, disrupting things. We've already had to cancel one show."

"We'll see where the investigation takes us."

Raffles paused at the next door. "Here we will spend some time getting to know the River Thames."

They entered a room plunged into semi-darkness. Projections along the wall showed images of the river.

A cheesy, mid-Atlantic voice boomed over loudspeakers. "Since the dawn of time, Old Father Thames has flowed through England, witnessing the birth of our great capital. Julius Caesar's invading army saw it as an obstacle, while the Vikings used it as a means to sail straight into the heart of England."

Shouts sounded on the audio track along with the voiceover: marauding Vikings, Diana supposed.

"The river was used for the disposal of waste for hundreds of years, leading to an event known as the Great Stink."

Diana heard a fan clicking into life and then smelled what seemed to be a blocked toilet mixed with rotten fish. She put a hand to her mouth, fighting her gag reflex.

Brie grabbed Raffles' arm. "Where are the toilets? I think I might vomit."

Raffles pointed towards a door. "Through there, second on the left."

Nearly everyone followed Brie. Raffles turned off the audiovisual display and spoke into a radio. "The smell's too much. I told you."

Sugarbrook turned to Diana. "This is dreadful," he whispered. "People pay money for this?"

She nodded. "All we can do is hope we're past the worst."

After a while, the group reassembled. Diana insisted on a window being opened and bottles of water being passed around.

"We're not allowed to open windows," Raffles told her.

"I don't care." She indicated a window on an end wall and Zaf reached up to open it.

Serena stepped forward, placing herself inches from Raffles' face. "Now, listen to me. I don't know what you do with non-VIP guests in this place, but I'm sure as hell ready to bail."

"I agree," said Charlotte. "Is there anything here that isn't a complete disaster?"

"Oh absolutely!" said Raffles. "Wait until you see the next experience. And after that, you can sample the delights of our cafeteria. On the house."

He grinned at the two women, but they'd already turned away.

Diana felt sorry for him. Where had Paul Kensington found him? He was probably on minimum wage.

"This way to meet the Pearly King and the Pearly Prime Minister," he said. "Come in here and please take a seat."

Diana held back in case any of the group made a run for it. But everyone filed inside.

Everyone except Zaf.

The room was laid out like a tiny theatre with bench seating and a small performance area. Wall displays showed Pearly Kings and Queens in outfits covered in mother-of-pearl buttons. Diana raised an eyebrow: she doubted this performance would do due honour to the Cockney tradition.

Distorted music blared over the loudspeakers: *Sweet Caroline*. Onstage, a man was doing what she supposed was intended to be a dance routine.

He was dressed head-to-toe in a suit decorated with buttons and he had a shocking blond wig. He held his arms crossed in front of him, while his legs galloped wildly.

Diana shook her head. Was this supposed to be Boris Johnson? She was almost embarrassed on Paul Kensington's behalf.

Almost.

There was a stage-whisper of "Lawnmower!" from offstage and the so-called Pearly Prime Minister switched to a stance which, Diana assumed, was supposed to represent someone pushing a lawnmower, all while walking in circles.

Another whisper of "Chicken!" was accompanied by funky chicken arms.

Diana put a hand up to her face: this was dreadful.

At last *Sweet Caroline* was replaced by the National Anthem. The Pearly Prime Minister stood to attention and Zaf stumbled onto the stage, dressed in robes and a crown decorated with buttons.

Diana peered around the tour group. They didn't look impressed.

The music changed again: *Dizzy* by The Wonder Stuff. The Pearly King started to dance, taking his lead from the Pearly Prime Minister and the whispered instructions from offstage.

Zaf gave it a good go. But Diana knew he wouldn't be happy after this.

"Is this what passes for tourism now?" said Sugarbrook.

"At least it's safer in here than on the lawless streets outside," replied Reuben.

Diana rolled her eyes. *Get me out of here.*

Chapter Fourteen

Charlotte leaned forward and tapped Diana on the shoulder. "This isn't the kind of entertainment we paid for."

"It's not ideal," Diana agreed.

The dancing ended and the lightest applause Diana had ever heard rippled around the group.

"I loved it," she heard Noah say to Brie. "As a songwriter you spend half your time worrying you're a hack and a fraud, but then I see something like this and I realise I'm really not that bad after all."

"Was that your young co-worker down there?" Serena asked Diana. "I admire his can-do attitude. But can you please take us back to the hotel? This place is a joke. Not even that. It's a waste of actual space."

Raffles appeared in front of them. "Don't go! Have

some lunch first. You might as well stay for something to eat."

Serena narrowed her eyes. "Will we be subjected to more nonsense?"

"Not really." Raffles didn't make eye contact.

"No. More. Nonsense." Serena jabbed a finger for emphasis. "Whatever nonsense is planned, cancel it now."

Raffles spoke into his radio. "Tell the *Austin Powers Groovy Hits of the Sixties* floor show to stand down."

Zaf joined them, having ditched his button-covered robes. He was flushed from dancing.

Diana gave him an amused smile and he frowned at her. "This didn't happen, alright?"

She nodded: *it didn't happen.*

They followed Raffles into a cafeteria. A large table was occupied by a dejected-looking group wearing psychedelic outfits in acidic shades. Diana wondered where they'd been recruited from.

"Groovy, Baby," said a man wearing oversized glasses as they walked past, but it was clear his heart wasn't in it.

"Are those Beefeaters serving burgers?" Zaf nodded at the serving staff behind the steel counters.

Diana followed his gaze. Could her heart sink any further?

"Why is that one wearing green?" she said. All of the Beefeaters except one were in the traditional red.

"His badge says vegan option," replied Zaf. "Plant-based Beefeater."

"Good grief."

"Honey, I know they made you take part in that awful song and dance routine," said Serena. "I admire the energy and dedication you put into it, in spite of it being a car crash. Here, this is for you." She slipped a bank note into the top pocket of his blazer.

"I can't take this just for doing some bad dancing, Ms McNash."

But Serena was already walking off, hand in the air. "I won't hear another word on the subject."

Zaf looked at Diana. "That's twice she's tipped me a fifty. That can't be right, surely?"

Brie leaned in. "She's a fan. Don't knock it unless it gets weird."

"Weird. Right." Zaf's expression suggested he thought this was already weird enough.

They made their way along the serving area. Most of the group chose the fish and chips, but then Diana spotted a dessert option at the end.

"No!" she said.

Zaf looked at her. "What's up?"

"Jellied eels. They've made it into a dessert."

"Looks like gummy worms."

"It does," she replied. "But that's not what jellied eels are."

"I've lived in London for twenty years," said Noah, "and I've never had them."

"Jellied eels are a proud London tradition," said Sugarbrook.

"Authentic London food," said Serena.

"Eels in jelly?" said Reuben.

Zaf turned to him. "Jelly means jam in America, right? It's not eels and jam, Mr Romano."

"What is it then?" asked the accountant.

Zaf shrugged.

"This needs fixing right now," said Diana. "Everyone, take your seats and try to put this morning's horrors out of your mind. I'm going to sort something out."

Chapter Fifteen

After lunch, they led the tour group back to the bus to find that Newton had eaten without them. Zaf eyed him; he'd heard rumours about bus drivers always being given the best food at tourist attractions.

Diana bent over Newton, muttering directions into his ear while Zaf shepherded the Americans onto the bus.

Once they were all safely on board, she grabbed the mic and turned to them.

"Not far to go for our alternative afternoon arrangements. If the Londiniumarium failed to give you a taste of the real London, it's because it lacks authenticity. I've asked a friend of mine to introduce you to somewhere truly authentic."

"Authenticity," Zaf heard Gareth say to Serena as

the bus pulled away. "I've always felt that it's my authenticity as a performer that's the key. I turned down the lead for that *Dick!* musical because it lacked authenticity. But this film role really leans into it. It'll be good publicity for the musical."

"The initial run is for four months," Serena replied, her tone clipped. "Evenings and matinees."

"I know that's what the contract says..."

Zaf left them to their argument and moved on down the bus. Their guests were perking up. Every mile they put between themselves and the Londiniumarium was a mile back towards sanity.

It was a short ride from Shoreditch to Limehouse. As they passed through Whitechapel, there was a Jack the Ripper-inspired stir among the Americans, despite the lack of foggy back alleys or Victorian urchins to feed their imaginations. Ten minutes later, they were driving over the Narrow Street swing bridge and entering Limehouse Basin. Newton pulled up outside a pub called the Duchess of Limehouse.

A bullet-headed, round-shouldered man was waiting outside. Zaf recognised him: Big Ernie.

Ernie tipped Zaf a nod. "'Allo, son." He walked round the bus to speak to Newton through the driver's window. "Once you've got 'em unloaded, pull into the yard at the side."

DCI Sugarbrook was watching him out of the window. "You have some interesting friends, Miss Bakewell."

She gave him a breezy smile as she led everyone off the bus and onto the pavement. Ernie stepped forwards and clasped her in a bear hug, then stepped back, looking Sugarbrook up and down.

"Well, if it isn't the old bill," Ernie said with a smile.

"Well, if it isn't the respectable face of organised crime," Sugarbrook replied.

Ernie sniffed. "I knew your old man, back in his boxing days. A man with a lot of respect."

"Probably a defence mechanism." Sugarbrook gave Ernie a disdainful look and went inside.

The pub was decorated with colourful tiles. Glazed vines of pastel green chased symmetrical flowers of light pink and yellow up and around the walls. Despite being at least a hundred years old by Zaf's reckoning, the tiles gleamed.

The bar was made of dark wood with a brass rail along the bottom. Tables of cast iron and mahogany were spaced around the room. Light filtered from outside through the stained-glass windows, and the smell of beer lingered in the air.

Ernie muttered in Diana's ear. She clapped her hands to get the group's attention.

"Everyone, welcome to the Duchess of Limehouse. My friend Ernie has arranged for us to use the function room. Follow me."

She led them through a door and up a narrow staircase lined with framed pictures of boxing stars from bygone eras. Zaf tried to see if he could spot Detective Sugarbrook's dad.

At the top of the stairs was a function room with its own bar and a row of windows overlooking the Thames.

"Oh, this is lovely!" said Serena.

Reuben looked uncertain. "Is that a balcony? It looks quite old."

"It's perfectly safe," Diana told him. "So, this room is ours, and we plan to keep things very simple. This is your opportunity to taste some proper London food. Soak up the views while we get that brought up."

The group drifted out onto the balcony, unable to ignore the view.

"Do I need to do anything?" Zaf asked Diana.

"Look after our guests," she said. "Ernie's sorting out the food, so you could help them choose drinks at the bar."

"Good idea."

He waited for the Americans to peel themselves away from the view and approach the bar. Reuben was first.

"I've heard plenty about British beer," the accountant said. "You have to drink it flat because the average Englishman drinks several pints a day."

Zaf had no idea how much beer the average person drank. "That sounds like a lot to me. I imagine you're talking about real ale or bitter. I don't think you have those in the US, do you?"

Reuben shrugged. "What are they?"

Zaf didn't have much of a taste for bitter. He thought he should probably be talking enthusiastically about hops, but didn't know where to start.

The barman leaned over. "How's about I pour you a drop of something? See how you like it."

"Please," said Reuben.

The shaven-headed barman took three glasses. Zaf watched him, trying to place him.

"First up," the barman said, "we'll try you on some bitter. See how it's hand pulled? I need to give it some muscle because we're drawing it off the barrel, see?"

Zaf had it: this was Chaz Chase, Ernie's right-hand man. Chaz had escorted him and Diana to a meeting with Ernie in a black cab when they'd been investigating a murder in the Houses of Parliament. Or at least, Zaf preferred to think of it as escorting rather than kidnapping.

Reuben took the glass and swirled it like he was tasting wine. "It's very dark." He took a sip and pulled a face. "Oh my." He stretched his lips back into a grimace.

Zaf looked at him. "Are you OK?"

Chaz held up a hand. "He'll be fine in a mo, that's normal. Now, yer gonna have to taste some stout or yer'll kick yerself. I bet you've heard of Guinness, right?"

Reuben nodded, his lips still twitching. "I have."

"Let's see how you like this one." Chaz set down

another glass. This one was ink-black with a creamy head on top.

"It's cute," Reuben said. "Looks like a fancy coffee." He took a sip and pulled a face, less extreme this time. "It's not terrible. Not terrible at all."

Chaz nodded in approval. "Now we'll go for a pale ale."

"This looks more like actual beer." Reuben held it up to the light.

"Don't be fooled," said the barman with a grin. "Full of flavour that is, compared with a lager."

Reuben gulped as he tasted it. His eyes widened. "Yes, it tastes quite different."

"So what's the verdict?" the barman asked. "Which one d'you prefer?"

Zaf was keen to know. He'd become quite invested in Reuben's journey into British beer.

Reuben sipped from each of the glasses again. "I feel as though the shock of the first one made the other two quite pleasant, but now I want to go back to the first one again. Is it wrong to be intrigued by something right on the cusp of being disgusting?"

"Not at all, mate." Chaz grinned. "Blandness is the enemy. So it's a pint of bitter, then?"

Reuben nodded. "Please."

As the barman pulled Reuben's pint, Brie and Serena joined them at the bar.

"I'll order you a white wine," Brie said to Serena.

Serena gave her disdainful look. "Why are you

trying to take all the fun away? Maybe I'd like to try some British beer. Did you ever think of that?"

"I was just—"

"Well don't."

Brie reddened and turned away. "I'll be back in a minute."

Serena smiled at the barman. "Could I please try some of those samples?"

"Right you are, sweetheart." Chaz began to pull more drinks.

Soon, he had sample drinks set up for most of the guests with no money taken from any of them. The alcohol and Chaz's easy-going manner relaxed the Americans, and the horrors of the morning were soon forgotten.

"There's great skill in being a barman," said Sugarbrook, just behind Zaf.

Zaf looked over his shoulder. "I'm not sure Chaz is a barman. But he's got a way with the punters."

Sugarbrook grunted. "If I showed you his police record, you'd have a very different opinion on how charming Chaz Chase is."

Serena McNash was next to Zaf, sipping a pint of bitter. He thought about the cash she'd tipped him, and the way she spoke to her PA.

He turned back to Sugarbrook. "People can be charming and horrible at the same time."

Chapter Sixteen

"Your boy the New York accountant is liking the bitter," muttered Ernie to Diana at the end of the bar. "He's on his third pint. Someone should tell him how strong it is."

"I'll let him know," she said. "But the chances of him listening if he's three pints in..."

Ernie pointed at Gareth. "I see you've brought TV royalty with you."

"He was in *Snoop!* Ridiculous detective nonsense."

"Tell me about it, love. I know a funny story about him an' all."

"Oh?"

"You know he had a stunt double for that show, right?"

"Did he? OK."

"Bloke's name's Terry if I recall right. Well anyway, he gets Terry to do some of the jobs a famous actor can't be seen doing. Terry would come over and purchase Mr Booncastle's Bolivian marching powder."

Diana frowned. "Gareth's a cocaine user?"

Ernie ignored the question. "Terry does his shopping as himself, as it were, and then when he gets back to the theatre, he does the old switcheroo, pops on a mop wig and slips inside in character as Gareth Booncastle. Classic, eh?"

Diana pulled back to look at Ernie. "Gareth got his stunt double to smuggle in his drugs?"

Ernie nodded. "I think they got a doorman in trouble when Gareth got lifted that one time for possession. Gawd knows how he was s'posed to tell the difference between the two of them, but there you are." He snorted. "I just remembered. Booncastle there got old Terry to take the rap for that possession charge. Paid 'im handsomely for it."

Diana remembered what Penny had overhead in the hotel. "What would happen if you ate cocaine?"

"Come again?"

"Ate it or drank it in a drink?" Diana said. "What would the symptoms be?"

Ernie opened his mouth then shut it again as he spotted DCI Sugarbrook approaching.

"I'm sure I wouldn't know, Diana," he said.

Sugarbrook gave Diana a cool look. "Symptons of cocaine consumption would include euphoria, anxiety,

restless energy and a lack of awareness of your sur-
roundings."

She remembered something Zaf had said. "Numb
hands?"

"Quite possibly. And, if taken in sufficient quantity, respiratory problems and maybe even a heart attack." Sugarbrook cocked his head. "Do you know
something I don't, Miss Bakewell?"

Big Ernie snorted. "You'd need a whole library to
write down all the things she knows that you don't."

"I'm just a good listener," Diana said.

Chapter Seventeen

Plates were being brought into the function room of the Duchess of Limehouse. Ernie clapped his hands.

"Right everybody! Now some of you might not be hungry, and some of you won't fancy the look of this, but do me a favour and listen for a minute, eh? We've got some proper traditional East End grub for you to try. Pie and mash with liquor and some jellied eels. The traditional thing would be to have a plate of pie, mash and liquor with some of the eels on a side dish."

Reuben put up a hand. He was swaying a little. "Are eels more like snakes or fish? And why the jelly?"

"Eels are fish, not snakes, squire. Look up what they get up to while they're alive, it'll blow yer socks off. Anyway, the jelly is what happens when they're cooked and cooled down, it's just gelatin from the bones. All natural."

Diana could see that Reuben's eyes were glazed. "Is the liquor very strong?" he asked.

Ernie gave him a smile. "Not that kind of liquor, chum. This is a sauce. It's flavoured with parsley and it's bloody gorgeous." He gave a chef's kiss that drew laughs. "Who's up for trying it? I'll serve you meself."

Diana smiled. Ernie rarely did this kind of thing himself; he had enough underlings for just about anything. But he'd been properly tickled at the challenge of showing these American visitors what London was all about.

Reuben stepped forward to try, followed by Serena.

"I 'eard you all had some sort of awful fake London carry-on," Ernie said as he started to load up plates. "I can't be doing wiv that sort of corporate claptrap. I bet it was all apples 'n pears."

"I don't think there was—" Reuben began.

"There were signs," said Brie. "The stairs were labelled 'apples n pears'."

"Oh," said Reuben. "I just assumed there were apples and pears upstairs."

Ernie slapped him on the back, laughing. Reuben coughed then walked away with his meal, a small pot of jellied eels quivering in his left hand.

"Cutlery over there," Ernie called to him. "Enjoy!"

Serena took hers, followed by the rest of the group.

Fifteen minutes later, almost everyone was eating and chatting.

"Care to get some eel inside you, Inspector?" said Ernie.

"I've eaten plenty of eel in my time," Sugarbrook replied. "Give me a chicken tikka masala any day."

"Can't say I disagree. It's good grub this, but it's hardly popular."

"We're here to give them an experience of London," Diana said. "And maybe enjoy some genuine East End culture while it still exists."

"As long as you don't expect me to do a Dick Van Dyke cockney," said Ernie. "Dance on the tables and make them think they're in some Hugh Grant *Notting Hill* version of London."

Diana eyed him. "Is Hugh Grant doing the Dick Van Dyke in this scene in your mind?"

"He's not wrong," Sugarbrook said. "Have you seen this *Cockney's Complaint* musical?"

"I've yet to have the pleasure," she replied.

"There may be a dancing chimney sweep or two." Sugarbrook registered the surprise on her face. "I took my two girls to see it. And as for that Gareth Booncastle's cockney accent..."

Diana nudged him in the ribs as Gareth came over, scraping up the last of his jellied eels from his plate.

"I like to think of myself as well-travelled," the actor said, "so how can it be that I've never tasted this particular delicacy?" He dug a spoon into his dish. "I always assumed there would be lots of bones. But it's just one bone in the middle, easy peasy!" He popped some into his mouth. "That is quite delicious. Slightly salty, quite mild, I love it."

Ernie nodded his approval.

Reuben had demolished his huge plateful and returned for more. He passed Diana on the way.

"This is great, thank you so much."

"Anything to lift the mood and get your business deal back on track," she said.

The accountant pulled a face. "I'm not so sure about the deal, but I appreciate the sentiment."

She frowned. "You don't think the deal's a good one?"

Reuben widened then narrowed his eyes. Diana watched him, wondering just how drunk he was.

"A good deal?" he said. "Financially? Heck, no."

"No?"

"It's a disaster. I'll keep running the numbers because that's what I'm paid for, but they haven't come up with anything that leaves us with an acceptable level of profit without significant risk. That *Dick!* musical lost the backers millions. You know only a quarter of all musicals make any money, and this one..."

He pulled a face of disdain.

"I'm sorry to hear that," Diana said. "I hadn't realised."

"The director's, er, accident would be the perfect excuse to call it off. But Serena's the only one who can make that call. Force majeure, et cetera. Either back straight out or claim it as an insurance write-off."

Sugarbrook had been listening. "Are you saying that Mr Granger's death might be beneficial?" he said in a quiet voice.

Reuben put his finger to his lips. He shrugged his shoulders, one then the other, then lurched towards the bar for another pint.

Chapter Eighteen

The sun was setting outside the pub's tall windows by the time everyone had finished eating.

Zaf surveyed the group. The Delphinium manager, Charlotte Webber, sat in a corner with the American accountant, deep in conversation. A bunch of actors from the London theatre were gathered in a loose circle, chatting loudly: *look at the fine time we're having here.* Serena McNash and a couple of others were enjoying the view from the balcony.

Zaf went to stand in the doorway. Across the river he could see Rotherhithe, with Canary Wharf and the Isle of Dogs along to the left. Zaf gazed at the skyscrapers, glinting in the low sun. One day they'd multiply so much they'd engulf the old East End completely.

He turned back inside and approached Brie and Noah Dart, sitting together in a corner.

"Can I join you?"

"If you can tolerate us reminiscing about the past," Noah said.

"A past I barely remember."

"My parents had this tiny place in Elephant and Castle," Brie said. "I remember Noah and Uncle Todd coming round, Noah on the piano. Me playing make-believe in princess dresses. A different world."

Noah leaned back and gestured at Brie. "Look at you now. Bigshot mover and shaker on Broadway."

She raised an eyebrow. "Mover of Serena's meeting times and occasional shaker of cocktails, maybe. A glorified secretary. But it's a step on the ladder. Step one, work for Serena. Step two, learn everything Serena knows."

"Step three, take Serena's job," said Noah.

Brie grunted a laugh.

"Tell me about Serena." Zaf dipped in his pocket for the fifty-pound note.

"Don't see many of them," Noah said.

"She's tipped me twice."

"Take the money and keep quiet."

"But I've done nothing. Nothing special. What's the deal?"

Brie patted his knee and smiled as if he'd been inducted into a special club. "She likes to own people. And she'd really like to own someone like you."

"Me?"

"Young, foreign and little bit cute."

Zaf coughed in surprise. "She's barking up the wrong tree there. I'm gay."

Brie rolled her eyes. "She's not *interested* in you. She just wants to add you to the collection."

There was a ragged cheer from the far corner of the room. Zaf looked over to see Diana whisking the cover off an upright piano. She pulled out a stool and lifted the lid.

"Can she play the piano?" asked Brie.

"No idea," Zaf replied.

"I can bang out a tune, same as a lot of people," Diana called. "I'm hoping someone more accomplished will take over if I start the ball rolling. Zaf, get over here."

Zaf gave Brie and Noah an apologetic shrug and joined Diana.

"I'm going to start singing," Diana said, "and I hope you'll join in."

Zaf opened his mouth to protest, but she was already playing scales.

Ernie approached them. "That's what's missing in boozers nowadays: a proper knees-up around the piano." He paced around the room. "If you've enjoyed the food I laid on, then yer can thank me by joining in with the songs. I'm a sucker for a singalong. We'll start with *It's a Long Way to Tipperary*, which is nice and easy. If you don't know the words, listen for the first part and then join in."

Zaf watched the puzzled expressions on the guests' faces.

In for a penny…

He drew in a deep breath. He knew this one, and he knew what his job was. Smiling, he walked to the centre of the room and raised his arms like a conductor.

Diana, still at the piano, gave him a wink and started playing. Zaf bellowed along as tunefully as he could, using gestures and making eye contact in an attempt to lure everyone else in.

Gareth Booncastle and a handful of other actors jumped up to join him. They powered through the song, and by the end of it most of the others had joined in.

"Great work, everybody," said Gareth. "We're just getting warmed up. Let's continue with another classic." He looked over at Diana. "Shall we *Roll Out the Barrel*, Diana?"

Zaf was relieved to see the group get through this one without his help. At the end, Noah Dart was steered towards the piano.

"I suppose we ought to give the actual composer a chance to play." Diana stood with a flourish, gesturing for Noah to take her place.

Noah sat down, frowned for a moment, then hammered out some swirling scales. He stopped as he struck a bum note.

He hit the key again and the piano emitted another off-key note.

Noah hit it again and again until it drew a laugh from the patrons. He shrugged then started playing with gusto. Zaf recognised the opening of *Voices of History* from *The Cockney's Complaint*.

The actors groaned, but then started to sing along. It was a solo, so the chorus of voices made it more powerful than when Zaf had heard it performed.

"I can't help but feel something primal when I hear this," said Brie, standing next to him. "It touches something so familiar inside me."

"Good music does that, right?"

"Noah always says there's no new songs, only new arrangements."

At the piano, Noah shifted to something livelier.

"*The Bow Bells Ring!*" he shouted: another song from the show. The group rose to their feet to sing and dance.

Chapter Nineteen

iana found Ernie in a quiet corner, smiling as he watched the group dancing.

"You pulled a blinder there, Ernie," she said. "This little taste of London has stolen their hearts."

"And so it should. We can't have 'em going back to the States thinking it's all plastic Beefeaters, can we?"

"Before I forget, I brought you some raspberries I picked from the garden square this morning." She reached into her bag and produced a carton.

Ernie inhaled. "Delicious. Cheers, Diana. And here's a little something for you."

He handed her a small baggie with *Herbs* written on the side in marker pen. It was filled with dry, shredded greenery.

"Thanks, Ernie."

Diana pocketed the cannabis, unashamed. She'd been smoking it ever since she'd arrived in London, back when people called it 'pot' rather than 'weed'.

Diana wasn't a big drinker, rarely gambled, certainly didn't touch the hard stuff like Gareth Booncastle. She didn't think this had done her any harm.

"So who do I send the bill for all this to?" Ernie asked, gesturing around the room.

Diana pulled a face. "Well, Paul Kensington was meant to be organising the day but Charlotte over there, the Delphinium manager, she's probably footing the bill. Although the money is ultimately coming from the American producer, Serena."

"Oh, she's got money to spare," Ernie said. "I reckon she could buy this pub with the small change in her back pocket."

"I'll sort it out," Diana told him.

He winked. "Maybe I'll go have a nice word with the American lady."

Charlotte Webber was standing in the centre of the room.

"Before you lot ruin your voices, the detective chief inspector has just informed me that we can open the theatre again tomorrow. We have work in the morning."

There were groans: the party was over. Noah thumped out a quick rendition of *Chopsticks* on the piano and closed the lid.

The guests filed dutifully onto the bus, all apart

from Sugarbrook who gave Diana a farewell nod and slipped into the Limehouse shadows. Charlotte had to help Reuben onto the bus.

"No being sick on the seats," Newton told him before starting the engine.

After depositing their guests at the hotel, Diana and Zaf strolled home from the bus depot. She was pleased they'd rescued what could have been a disastrous day, with Ernie's help.

"That pie, mash and eels was really nice," Zaf said. "Why haven't we done that on all our tours?"

Diana laughed. "Say 'eels' to someone, and they start to get a bit squeamish. But everyone who's tried it has liked it." She gave Zaf a sidelong glance. "I'm still peckish, though. I think I'll eat the rest of the salad in the fridge."

Zaf sucked his teeth.

"The salad with the grated carrot and cumin?" he asked after a pause. "I... I thought that was just a snack that was up for grabs."

"You ate it."

"It was really nice," he said. "I mean, I'm really sorry, but it's a testament to your cooking."

"You're a troublesome flatmate, Zaf Williams."

"It's not deliberate."

"Doesn't make it better."

At the flat, Zaf went straight into his room while Diana went to the kitchen. She was planning on making hash brownies with the weed she'd got from Ernie.

She made a double batch: hash brownies and regular brownies. She knew from experience that only having hash brownies around the flat could be a recipe for disaster. Finally, she threw in a good spoonful of mixed spice for extra flavour.

While the brownies were cooking, Diana went out for a walk. Early evening was a lovely time to wander the garden square, with its little paths and neat beds of dense plantings. She knew many of the plants were edible, and nibbled a frond of Sweet Cicely as she passed.

She greeted a group of her neighbours enjoying a game of tennis on one of the courts. She and Zaf had talked about having a game. Maybe it would be a good way to work out some of their differences.

Back at the flat, she took the brownies out of the oven. The scent filled the air, and she was surprised Zaf hadn't appeared to ask for any. When she glanced at her phone, she saw he'd texted her while she'd been in the square, to let her know he'd gone out with friends.

"Fair enough," she said to the empty flat.

She had a brownie with a cup of tea and settled down to watch the square from her favourite chair.

There was lots to think about: from the awful death in the theatre, all the way through to Paul Kensington's continuing stupidity, via the still-missing Gus.

At last it was time for bed. She tidied up her plate, wondering how late Zaf would be back. The early hours, no doubt. And he'd be hungry.

She boxed up the brownies into two separate containers, put the containers in the fridge, and placed a note between them.

Eat these ->
    <- Don't eat these

She stepped back and checked. That should be clear enough.

Chapter Twenty

Zaf reckoned he'd perfected the art of sneaking in late.

It was all well and good trying to be super quiet, teasing the lock open, creeping along the hallway and pulling the bedroom door shut in complete silence. But there came a point where trying to stay quiet meant making even more noise.

No: the true expert entered with a silent, stealthy rhythm. Cool, slow and graceful.

He'd spent the night dancing at a new backstreet club, just what he needed after such a weird day. If someone had told him when he'd come to London that he'd perform as a Pearly King and lead an old-fashioned sing-song, he'd have laughed. Going clubbing had reminded him he wasn't secretly middle-aged.

Diana had left brownies in the fridge. He read the note between them. It made no sense.

Shrugging, he grabbed a brownie and headed to bed.

When he woke, Diana had already left and the flat was quiet. He grabbed a quick shower, aware he was already running late.

He was hungry. There was no time for breakfast.

And there were brownies in the fridge.

Zaf grabbed one of the containers and stuffed it in his rucksack. He read the note again – eat these, not these – and was confident she'd be OK with him taking a box.

As Zaf entered the depot, he could hear Paul Kensington shouting. The door to his office was closed, but it was clear that Diana was getting some serious flack for yesterday's events at the Londiniumarium.

Paul wasn't an imposing boss: he was more irritating than frightening. But Zaf wondered if he should go in and back her up. Maybe tell Paul how awful (and unpronounceable) the Londiniumarium was.

While he was steeling himself to go in, the door opened and Diana stepped out.

Newton looked up from polishing the front of the bus. "What happened?"

Diana shrugged. "Paul is keen for the Londiniumarium to work. He was... disappointed that we'd left early."

"I meant, did he say anything about me requesting the day off to go looking for Gus?"

Diana frowned at him.

Zaf shook his head. "That whole Londiddy-doodle-um place is bad."

"He doesn't want to hear that," Diana said. "He might be more than a little personally invested."

"Financially?"

She shrugged. "He was pleased to hear about you stepping in as a Pearly King. Well done for that."

"Pfft." Zaf never wanted to speak of it again.

"And he's had a call from Charlotte Webber," Diana continued. "She's told him never to send her group anywhere near the place again. In fact, she told him how much she enjoyed the alternative arrangements yesterday afternoon."

Zaf grinned, then saw Diana's expression. "I bet that made him ever madder."

"It did." She shook her head. "He's left the rest of the tour in our hands. He's washing his hands of the whole thing. I need to come up with something."

"*We* need to come up with something," said Zaf. He beckoned Newton over.

"I'm not doing a group hug." Newton held his hands up. "I can't think of anything but Gus at a time like this."

"OK, no hugs," said Zaf. "But let's see what we can come think of, so it's not all up to Diana."

Zaf went to the kitchen and put the kettle on.

They still had time before they were due to collect the guests from the Redhouse Hotel.

"We need to lay on a trip that really sells London to the Americans," he told Diana as she sat at the kitchen table.

"But one that doesn't cost the earth," she said. "Paul forked out for that awful thing yesterday. I'm still not sure who'll foot the bill for the pie and eels."

Zaf poured two mugs of tea. "How about a walking tour of famous movie locations. *Notting Hill, Four Weddings, Love Actually.*"

"That's very Hugh Grant-themed," said Diana. "I hear ACE Tours are doing Bridget Jones' Diary themed weekends. Potentially inexpensive."

"No good if you're not actually a rom-com fan."

Diana pursed her lips. "My friend Carolyn does a guided exploration of the Thames foreshore."

"Isn't that just wading around in the mud?"

"And looking for treasure."

"We're trying to grease the wheels of a theatre deal, Diana. Are we really selling London to the Americans if they're up to their knees in muck?"

"It's called mudlarking," she said. "We're selling them London's rich history. Besides, don't you get the impression that not everyone wants the deal to go ahead?"

"How d'you mean?"

Diana sat down. "I spoke to Reuben, the accountant, while we were in the pub."

Zaf nodded, then winced. He rubbed his head.

"Are you alright?" she said. "You seem a bit... woozy."

"Out late." He shrugged. He was feeling dodgier than usual, but he didn't want Diana thinking he couldn't hack it. "Sorry. Carry on."

"I don't think he would have said anything to me," she continued, "but he was somewhat worse the wear from all the bitter Chaz served him. He told me the deal was a financial disaster."

"But he's the accountant," Zaf said. "Surely it's his job to make it work, moneywise?"

"That's what you'd expect. But he didn't seem to think it was a good idea."

Zaf leaned back in his chair, hoping to get more comfortable. "I get the feeling there's a lot going on in that group that they're not telling us about."

"There are plenty of opinions and private motives."

"Motives to kill Todd Granger?"

She shook her head. "Just motives. Although... Reuben did say that Todd's death might make it easier for the Americans to back out, if they wanted to. But that's not what I mean. I mean they all have different motives. Motives to be here, motives to be involved in the production... and yes, maybe motives to kill. It's difficult to—"

"What?" Zaf said. "Todd's death... do you really think it wasn't an accident?"

"The police wouldn't be showing an interest if it was entirely innocent."

Zaf nodded and sipped his tea. He'd piled five sugars into it, hoping it would help.

"DCI Sugarbrook certainly showed an interest in the group."

Diana raised an eyebrow. "I asked him about it. I thought it was odd, a detective spending half the day on a bus tour."

Zaf grinned. "Skiving. And remember, it was you that invited him."

"Indeed. He was observing, or so he told me. I think he agreed to the idea because he thought that quietly tagging along would allow him to watch the group and see if anyone was behaving oddly."

"So, he thinks it was murder."

"It looks like it."

Zaf looked at her, thinking back. "What was it they said? *Vast quantities of cocaine in his bloodstream.* But no one seems to think Todd was a regular user."

"Unlike our actor friend, Gareth."

"An actor doing cocaine? That's a bit of a cliché."

Diana nodded. "But Todd had definitely taken something. Plenty of people spotted the effect on him. He was buzzing, agitated."

"That woman from the crew told me he'd said his hands were numb."

"I remembered you saying that. I told Sugarbrook.

He was very interested in what Todd had been drinking before his death. The big, colourful cocktail."

Zaf rubbed between his eyes. The wooziness was wearing off, but only slightly. Why was he feeling like this?

"Can you get someone to drink a load of cocaine without noticing?" he asked.

"Maybe if you mask the bitter taste with sugar."

Zaf looked at his mug of tea and then at Diana. "How do you know what cocaine tastes like?"

She raised an eyebrow. "I might be a woman of a certain age. I'm not a nun, Zaf."

Chapter Twenty-One

"So, if Todd hadn't fallen from the light rigging, he could well have died from a heart attack anyway," Zaf said as they went to join Newton at the bus.

"Which begs the question of what he was doing up there," replied Diana, stepping her way around a pot of cleaning fluid.

"I was up there, too."

"Yes, what were you doing up there?"

"Trying to find my way back to the party. Stupid Gus getting me into bother."

"I'm so worried about him," said Newton.

Diana turned to the driver. "He's a big boy. He'll cope for now."

Newton shook his head. Were his eyes red?

It's just a cat, Diana thought. A cat they'd all

grown very attached to, but still. He'd been a stray, before coming to Chartwell and Crouch...

"I wasn't up in the lights, obviously," Zaf said. "But I was up on that level, by the technical booth." He raised a finger. "Todd's empty glass was in the technical booth. He'd been in there."

"Maybe it was confusion that made him go up to the light gantry. Cocaine can have that kind of effect."

Zaf gave her a puzzled look. "You think someone put the cocaine in his drink to kill him?"

She scratched her chin. "Who would want to kill Todd Granger? He seemed to be well-liked. A respected theatre director with a wide circle of friends."

"An old family friend of Brie's, too," Zaf said. "I saw her face when she met up with him after so long. His, too. He was going to give her a gift or something before he went and died."

Diana nodded. "If I was looking for a motive, I'd be exploring the fact that he was integral to the US deal. He was going to America to direct their production."

"Kill the American show by killing the director? So, someone hates the show? Hates the Americans?"

Diana wasn't sure. "Or perhaps someone wants to save the British show from losing its talent, including Gareth Booncastle. Or wants to save the Americans' money by killing the Broadway version before it's born." She grunted. "The Delphinium has a sobering reminder of what can go wrong across the street. That Dick Whittington musical."

"*Dick!*"

"Yes. With an exclamation mark, like that might improve it. I don't think it lasted more than a fortnight."

"I thought all those shows ran for years."

"Not necessarily," said Diana, "So if we assume that stopping the deal was the reason for killing Todd, we might argue that the theatre manager, Charlotte, the American producer, Serena, or even her accountant, Reuben, have a motive."

"Or Gareth."

Diana looked at Zaf. "Really? Surely, a move Stateside would be good for his career."

"I've heard him talking about a film role a couple of times."

"He wants to back out of his contract and go off to Hollywood?"

"Maybe. And, like you said, he's got access to cocaine."

Diana drew in a breath. She could hear Newton, on the other side of the bus, muttering something. Was he calling for the cat?

"He was nervous," she said, "about Sugarbrook poking around at the Delphinium. He stayed close to the detective all day yesterday. I thought that was an actor fishing for source material, but it might be guilt."

"Or paranoia."

"Or paranoia," she agreed.

Newton reappeared at the side of the bus. He

picked up the cleaning fluid and placed it in a cupboard, locking it and pocketing the key. He turned to them. "I like to keep things ship-shape."

"And we appreciate it, Newton," she said.

They had enough to focus on, with the threats to Chartwell and Crouch: the Londiniumarium and the awful uniforms Paul Kensington was planning.

Did she have the time or headspace to be thinking about murder? Surely that was Sugarbrook's job?

But Sugarbrook had missed the clues completely when poor Florence Breecher had died in the Houses of Parliament. Diana and Zaf had juggled guiding their group of school students with working out the truth.

And once again, Diana's natural curiosity was getting the better of her.

"So," she said, "one of them put cocaine in Gareth's drink. Enough to kill him or at least to make him unaware of what he was doing. The police will be trying to work out who had access to Todd's drink—"

"And cocaine," added Zaf.

"In the minutes before his death."

Chapter Twenty-Two

Zaf was thinking about Todd Granger's death as the bus headed towards the hotel to pick up the US visitors. He was still thinking about it when he went inside to meet the group.

Down the long corridor leading from reception to the restaurant, he saw Reuben Romano and Charlotte Webber close together, talking. He paused, narrowing his eyes. Should he be suspicious of them?

They saw Zaf and stepped apart. Charlotte reached out a hand as if she was about to give Reuben something, glanced at Zaf again, and pulled her hand back. She retreated through a patio door to the rear gardens, her movements jerky.

Reuben glanced at Zaf, then towards the direction Charlotte had disappeared in. He looked down at the carpet. At last, he pushed his shoulders back and walked towards reception, approaching Penny.

"I need to find a drugstore," he said.

"Drugstore?" Zaf's mind went to what Diana had been saying about cocaine.

"A pharmacy?" said Penny. "There's a Boots on Baker Street. And another one further down Crawford Street."

"How many blocks walk is that?"

She pulled a face. "We don't really have blocks here."

"I thought the maps were all screwy. So how do they work then, the streets?" Reuben cocked his head. "Who decides where they go?"

Penny shrugged. "Well, a lot of the roads go back hundreds of years. Laid out by Tudors or Romans or—"

"Romans?" Reuben's face lit up.

"Er, yes. There are some Roman roads in London."

"The Shoreditch High Street we drove along yesterday was a Roman road," said Zaf.

"Laid down by my forebears?" Reuben said, a note of wonder in his voice.

Zaf smiled. It was like Reuben had just been told he was a wizard and had been accepted into Hogwarts.

"I think your transportation might be ready." Penny indicated Zaf.

"No," said Reuben. "No tours this morning. We

have a Zoom at ten with the bank." He gave Zaf a serious look. "This is a business trip."

"OK," said Zaf. "And Serena and the others...?"

"Finishing off breakfast, and then the Zoom." The accountant took a step towards the door. "Pharmacy on Baker Street? An indeterminate number of blocks. Got it."

As he left, Zaf turned to Penny. "I just saw Charlotte go into the garden."

"Who?"

"The theatre manager. English woman. Did she come in to talk to Reuben?"

Penny gave him a puzzled look.

"I'm just curious," he said. "Wondered what they were talking about."

She raised an eyebrow. "You want me to tell you about the confidential comings and goings of our guests, Zaf?"

Zaf leaned in, hoping she was just messing with him. They were interrupted by Noah Dart coming in from the street.

He put both hands on the counter. "Can you tell me what room Brie Grebbson is in?"

"Would you like me to call her?" asked Penny.

"No, no. I don't want to disturb her. There's just this gift thing and—"

"A gift?" said Brie, suddenly at his elbow.

"My, what a busy reception desk I've got this morning," said Penny.

Serena wasn't far behind Brie. She smiled at Zaf.

"My darling Zaf. I'm sure you had all manner of delights lined up for us, but there's a change of plan today."

"You've got a Zoom meeting at ten with the bank," said Zaf.

"Psychic as well as handsome." Serena's cheek dimpled.

"Um, is everything OK?" said Noah. "With the bank, I mean?"

"It's all just numbers," said Serena, her gaze still on Zaf. "Todd's death changes things."

"Noah," Brie said, "you said something about a gift?"

"For Todd," explained Noah. "Well, his family. Charlotte thought it would be a nice gesture."

"For his ex?" Brie asked.

"They were still close."

"So, some flowers?"

"Oh, think big, Brie," said Serena. "The man was a giant of theatre. We're in London. Harrods. Fortnum and Mason."

"Fortnum and Mason do really nice hampers, I hear," said Zaf.

Brie looked at him. "A bereavement hamper, is that a thing?"

"It is now," said Serena. "Brie can do that."

Brie looked at her boss.

"I don't need you for the Zoom," Serena said, with

just enough of a pause after *don't need you* to make her opinion of Brie clear.

"OK, right," said Brie. "Bereavement hamper. Not sure where to start."

"I'll jot down some ideas," said Noah. "Help you find the very best items."

"And maybe Zaf here can help you," said Serena.

"I—" began Zaf.

"You are our tour guide, aren't you?" purred the American producer.

"I am."

"Then guide Brie here. Teach her a thing or two."

"Is no one going on the tour today then?" he asked.

"I've got things to do here," said Noah. "Rehearsals are in full swing at the Delph. Here." He pushed a piece of paper with a scribbled list towards Zaf.

"A hamper, then," said Serena. "And I will see you later, young man."

Slightly bewildered, Zaf stepped outside with Brie. Diana was waiting on the pavement in front of the Routemaster bus.

"You seem to be short of a few guests today," she said.

"Tour's off, apparently."

"Completely?"

Zaf indicated Brie. "I've offered to help Brie buy a bereavement hamper for Todd's family."

"Is that a thing?"

"Apparently it is," said Brie.

Diana nodded. "Then I will go to the theatre."

"To look for Gus?" called Newton from inside the bus.

"Among other things," said Diana. "There are things I want to look at."

Zaf could see a sly twinkle in her eye.

Chapter Twenty-Three

Zaf and Brie caught the Bakerloo line underground from Baker Street to Piccadilly Circus. They stood gripping the pole in the aisle, swaying with the movement of the train.

"My parents' place was along the Bakerloo line," said Brie. "Elephant and Castle. Do you know it?"

"Know of it." Zaf noticed a faraway look on her face. "Want to go check it out?"

"Maybe," she said. "How far is Elephant and Castle?"

He looked over at the tube map on the wall of the carriage. "Ten minutes. We going to check out where you lived as child?"

"Have we got time?"

"We can make time."

They continued past Piccadilly Circus and the crowd thinned. Zaf indicated two seats and they sat down, Brie's eyes on the tube map above the people opposite. Zaf had been in London for a couple of years now and no longer had to keep his eye on the map all the time.

He dipped into his bag and pulled out the box of brownies. He held it out to Brie. "Brownie?"

"You always carry cake on you?"

"I was in a hurry, so I grabbed these on the way out. They're homemade."

"You bake?"

He shook his head. "Diana." He eyed the brownies. They looked delicious. "I'm having at least two."

"They look pretty good." Brie reached over and took a large one, making appreciative noises as she ate it.

At Elephant and Castle they exited the station at a busy roundabout and crossed to a plaza area surrounded by roads.

"Do you remember where you used to live?" Zaf asked.

"A turning off Rodney Road," said Brie. She held out a hand, then dropped it. "Huh. I barely recognise any of this."

"London changes constantly."

"Memory changes constantly." Brie looked around, then seemed to fix on something. Come on."

Zaf followed her, trying to ignore the din of traffic around them. He was glad this wasn't a spot on his usual walk home from the depot.

As they walked, Brie talked, repeatedly leaning in towards Zaf. "I think we inflate the idea of places and people in our memories. Take this place, Elephant and Castle. With a name like that, you'd think it's somewhere magical, somewhere strange. Why's it called Elephant and Castle, anyhow?"

"I know that one," said Zaf. "Well, as much as anyone does. They reckon it's a mispronunciation of *La Infante de Castilla*. That's Eleanor of Castile. "

"Excellent Spanish there, Zaf."

He grinned. "It's a myth though, most likely."

"It is?"

He shrugged. "Probably just named after an old pub."

Brie laughed. "That sounds more London. I prefer the Spanish princess idea."

A few minutes later, she pointed towards a side road. "Here."

"Here?"

"Here."

Munton Road was an unassuming street bordered by a park on one side and apartment buildings on the other.

"Up there, I think." Her finger aimed at a second-floor balcony. "I have very strong but hazy memories. Does that make sense?"

"Everything makes sense to me right now." Zaf felt woozy, like the world was settling into a deep cosy cushion around him.

"This was back when my dad was alive, when my parents were together. I have these memories of a home, of a bedroom, a house filled..." She laughed. "It really was a house filled with music and laughter. That's what I remember. And since my dad had no parents and my mom's family were back in Canada, my extended family was their friends. A lot of musicians and actors. I loved them. Maybe now I'd think half of them were slackers and dreamers."

"Nothing wrong with being a dreamer."

"Unless you don't have the will to pursue that dream. Dad was always writing songs. He'd record them, sometimes with one of those old flip video things. I thought I was the star of the show, obviously, and they never told me otherwise."

"That's what loving parents do," said Zaf. "My mum is still super protective of me, even though she's a hundred miles away. She complains I don't talk to her as much as my sister does. I reckon Connie's boyfriend Rav is worming his way in to becoming number one son in mum's eyes. He's a crime scene investigator."

"CSI London?" Brie put a hand on Zaf's arm.

"Birmingham. I wonder what he'd make of this death at the theatre thing." Zaf realised what he'd said. "I'm sorry. I wasn't thinking. My brain..."

Brie shook her head. "It's OK. There's nothing

normal about this situation." She sighed. "And we leave so much left unsaid: threads dangling, words unspoken."

She turned away from the block of flats, her face full of sadness.

Chapter Twenty-Four

Diana and Newton's walk from the depot to the Delphinium took them along Oxford Street and through the growing throngs of shoppers, then along Regent Street with its broad curving sweep and impressive Georgian architecture. At Piccadilly Circus the crowds thickened again and they stopped at the first of many pedestrian crossings leading them London's West End.

"I'm not saying I don't care about Gus," said Diana, her eyes on the red man. "He's a perfectly charming moggy. But he was a street cat before he came to live with us and if that big ball of fluff has been able to look after himself all these years, then he'll probably be fine."

The red man was replaced by the green 'walk' man

and they pushed across, surrounded by crowds of tourists.

"But he's got used to us being around for him," Newton said.

"*You've* got used to having him around," Diana said, realising she was only partly right. She'd got used to Gus too.

Diana had known plenty of cats and dogs in her time (and a few budgies, parrots and tortoises) and although she wouldn't have called herself a pet person, she recognised how important they could be in people's lives. Especially in a city like London. where it could be hard to build relationships.

"We'll find him, I'm sure," she said as they crossed a second crossing towards theatreland.

Newton grunted, unconvinced. They continued in silence, taking two more crossings and then looping round to the Delphinium. Their route took them past the Lyric, the Gielgud and the Sondheim theatres. Diana wondered if the real-life events in those theatres were as dramatic as those that had taken place among her tour group, or if the drama was confined to the stage.

The front doors to the theatre were locked.

Before Newton could complain, Diana headed up the narrow side street to the stage door entrance. A man in a formal suit was at the stage door.

Diana smiled, recognising him. "Farrell Adesina."

"Miss Diana Bakewell." Farrell was ten years older

than Diana, but his smile seemed to make him ten years younger.

"My young colleague Zaf told me he'd had a run-in with a stern but devilishly handsome doorman. I had no idea it was you."

"That the young man who lost his cat by any chance?" said Farrell. "You tell him he can't leave it in here, you know."

"You've seen Gus?" Newton's eyes were wide.

"This is my other colleague," Diana said. "Newton Crombie."

"Newton." Farrell reached out to envelop Newton's hand in his massive fist. "That your cat in there?"

"He sort of belongs to the depot... but yes."

"Well, I'd like to see that cat back at your depot and out of my theatre."

"Me too. If I could...?" Newton gestured at the door.

Farrell pulled it open. "I'll radio Marina on reception. Let her know you're coming through. Don't go disturbing the rehearsals."

Newton ducked through the door, bowing with gratitude.

Diana knew Farrell from her days working in a recording studio in St John's Wood. She'd seen him move through a number of jobs since, always with customers, often door work.

"I was due to take the tour group out today," she

told him, "but I think they've been diverted into other things."

"Rehearsals," said Farrell. "They know that thing backwards and forwards. I can whistle the tunes in my sleep."

"The old grey whistle test," she replied.

"Less of the old and grey, you cheeky girl." He stroked his shiny brown scalp. "They're just spooked. The death of that Todd has got them doubting themselves."

That Todd. Diana cocked her head.

"What did you think of Todd Granger?"

Farrell pursed his lips. "A tiny, self-important tyrant of a man. But that's all directors, isn't it?" He shook his head. "He was alright, I suppose. But he did try to have me fired that time."

"Oh?"

"Mr Booncastle was playing silly buggers with his stunt double from his detective show. People sneaking about. That Todd made out it was all my fault." He held out his hands. "But I didn't kill him. I've been known to break a leg or two, but I believe in tolerance and forgiveness. It's the only way to swim with the sharks, you know."

Farrell had worked the doors in some of the worst nightclubs and bars in Soho. He'd doled out tolerance and forgiveness with his fists more than a few times.

"If you go inside and promise to behave," he said, "you can listen to Mrs Webber and the assistant director tearing strips off Mr Booncastle for his efforts in today's rehearsal. It's sweet music."

He held open the stage door.

"Thanks." Diana stepped inside.

As soon as the door closed behind her, she heard the shouting. It came from along a corridor backstage.

Meanwhile onstage, someone was calling for people to go back to starting positions. The music began and someone sang the opening refrain of *Goodbye Old London Town*.

Diana felt like she was sneaking around. She'd even adopted a slight crouch. She looked at her duck's head brolly.

"Mr Booncastle is on stage," she whispered. "No better time to call into his dressing room."

She crept down the side of the stage. A woman in a headset sat at the prompt desk. As Diana approached, she gave an inquisitive look.

Diana smiled.

Look like you're supposed to be here, she told herself. That generally worked.

She adopted a more confident stride and passed the woman, heading for the dressing rooms.

There were two lead actor dressing rooms either side of a rough wooden door, with a gold star on the door of Gareth Booncastle's.

A gold star. Why was Diana not surprised?

"How nice," she said as she slipped inside.

Chapter Twenty-Five

On the journey back to Piccadilly Circus, the noises of the train reverberating through Zaf's head sounded even louder than normal. He slumped in his seat, wondering why his skull felt paper-thin.

Piccadilly was busy with people, some in a hurry and some lingering to soak up the sights: the hoardings, the lights, the famous statue.

Brie turned to Zaf as they waited for yet another green man to light up. "Do you like being a tour guide?"

"I love it," said Zaf. "It's fun being with so many different people. I know we're supposed to be educating the guests on the sights of London, but I'm learning things all the time. About London, and about people."

The lights changed and they started to walk, ignoring the jostles from the crowd around them.

"I get that," she said. "Some people are energised by being around other people. You're like that."

"I like working with Diana, too," he said. "I'll never know as much as she does, but if I hang around with her for long enough, some of it'll make its way into my head." He put a hand to his head, miming the act of squashing knowledge into it, then winced: his head was throbbing.

Brie laughed. Zaf joined her. A little part of his brain told him it wasn't funny, but he couldn't help himself.

Brie made shapes in the air as they reached the other side of the road. "Woo! Knowledge! Comin' atcha!"

Zaf playfully patted her hands away and she leaned into him.

"Want some tourist stuff?" he said. "Look. See that statue."

Brie blinked her eyes rapidly and stared at the statue on its plinth. "Eros."

Zaf shook his head. He knew this one. "It's actually Anteros, the god of selfless love."

"Isn't that what Eros is?"

Zaf looked up at the metal statue of the winged god with his bow. He thought back to a conversation he and Diana had had a few weeks ago as they passed through here. "Eros was the god of love and, y'know, that kind of stuff. But he was a boy. Permanently, a boy. So the gods gave him a brother, Anteros. The idea was that Anteros' selfless love would help Eros to grow. But whenever Anteros went away, Eros shrank back to being a child."

"I think I know some people like that," said Brie.

Zaf nodded. "We all rely on each other."

"And some people feed off others. I know plenty of emotional vampires."

They walked west along the wide, almost boulevard-like Piccadilly, eating a second or possibly third brownie as they went.

"Ooh look, Fortnum and Mason," said Zaf.

"Do the tour guide thing then," said Brie. "What d'you call that style?"

Zaf looked up. He knew he'd get away with saying it was Georgian, even though he wasn't sure. But did she mean the decoration?

"The pale green and gold with lots of curly corners and fancy plaques?" he said.

Brie nodded, giggling.

Zaf stroked his chin, imagining himself as a professor of buildings. "I do believe we have a classic example of wedding cake architecture here."

"Wedding cake, yes!" Brie laughed. "Let's go inside and see if it's made from fruit cake."

Laughing at their own hilariousness, they went in. The interior was light and airy.

"Aha," said Zaf, "we have more wedding cake architecture inside. See how the ceilings look like icing?"

The two of them looked up, swaying as they turned in a circle staring at the ceiling. The centre of the exclusive food shop was dominated by an open well that ran from the basement all the way up to the ornate ceiling several floors above.

"Icing, yeah. It looks a bit yummy." Brie sighed. "I don't want to do this, really."

"Yeah?"

"It's such a nice day. Let's go chill in a park or something."

"Oh, yeah." Zaf could feel a gentle tiredness seeping through him.

Brie leaned into him, putting her hand on his chest. He was glad to be able to lean back against her for the support.

"Park later," he said. "For now, we'll get the things for the hamper, no problemo."

"No problem."

"*No problemo, mi amiga.*"

Brie smiled at him. "You *do* speak Spanish."

"I speak all the languages." Zaf knew that wasn't true but in that moment, it kind of felt like it was. "Now, where's that list?"

"What list?" Brie's voice was slurring now.

"The list. The list list. The food list."

Brie nodded. "No problem." She fumbled in her

bag, then checked her pockets. "Small *problemo*. I think I list the lost."

"You list the lost?"

"I said I list the lost. Pay attention." She frowned. "Can you remember any of the things that were on it?"

"Not really. I glanced through it and thought it all sounded very fancy."

"Very fancy, then! Let's go find some fancy stuff."

"This might be the best shopping trip ever. We don't need a list."

"Or a lost."

"That too," Zaf said. "I think we can just intuit what we need."

"Intuit?"

"Like one of them geezers with the thingies." He tried to mime a water diviner with divining sticks.

"Geezer thingies." Brie nodded, her expression solemn.

Zaf went to the nearest display.

"Biscuits?" said Brie. "You intuited biscuits."

He picked a tartan-patterned pack of biscuits off the shelf. "With my geezer thingies. Biscuits! Who doesn't want biscuits?"

"We need a basket," said Brie. "We might need to get some biscuits for the hamper and some to eat on our way round."

"A biscuit basket?"

"A biscuit basket. And nibbles."

"Great idea," said Zaf. "In fact, let's do that for

everything, then we'll be able to tell if it's fancy enough."

"Genius. It's this sort of attention to detail that makes us great at our jobs, Zaf." Brie laughed.

"You're amazing at your job," he said.

"No, *you're* amazing," she replied. "Don't let anyone tell you otherwise. Now, are florentines the same as biscuits?"

Zaf peered at the pack. "Only one way to be sure. Let's open this one and try them." He pulled the end of the packet open and slid out a plastic tray. "You don't get many!"

Brie took one. "Definitely a biscuit. Nice, too. It's not quite a brownie, though. Got any more of them?"

The two of them finished off the last bits of brownie, leaving more room in Zaf's bag for fancy food stuff.

Chapter Twenty-Six

areth Booncastle's dressing room in the Delphinium was bigger than a cupboard but only just. It was a room in the same way that estate agents described a tiny box room at the back of a house as a third bedroom.

There was a dressing table with the obligatory backlit mirror, a lounging chair with a tiny table and, at the back, a rack for clothes. There was a champagne bucket, with three inches of water standing in it.

Diana sat at the stool in front of the mirror. She regarded her reflection.

"I am Gareth Booncastle, TV star and stalwart of the stage."

She smiled at herself, trying to immerse herself in the role of Gareth. She threw back imaginary curly locks.

"I have a cocaine habit, according to Big Ernie. I also have a habit of playing pranks with my stunt double, pranks that get the doorman into trouble. I should be pleased that *Cockney's Complaint* is moving to Broadway but perhaps I want to do that Hollywood movie instead."

There were various papers on the dressing table. Diana rifled through them, hoping for an audition script for a Spielberg movie or something like that. Was the lure of Hollywood enough motivation for Gareth to kill Todd, just to scupper the transatlantic deal?

There were printed-off plane tickets and a letter from Gareth's agent about royalties and residuals. But no film script. There was a post-it note on which someone, presumably Noah Dart, had written *Take a look, Gareth. I think you could really rescue this one, Noah.* Under that someone, possibly Gareth, had written *Heck no, Noah. No, Noah. Noah, no* and drawn a smiley face.

A scrap of plastic on the edge of the dresser caught her eye. It was the torn corner of a plastic bag, with a small quantity of white powder tucked into it.

"Tut tut, Mr Booncastle."

Next to the bag was the tiniest cluster of powder crumbs. Diana looked closer, to see that they continued like scattered stars across the carpet towards the waste bin.

She went to the bin and crouched. One edge of the

bin was taken up with a thick script, printed on A4. But this was no Hollywood film script. In bold letters on the front were the words *Dick! – A Musical.*

Intrigued, Diana was about to lift it out when there came a cry from beyond the wall, followed by a crash.

She stood, suddenly afraid of being caught snooping, as well as worried about what she'd just heard.

She went to the door, checked if anyone was about, then hurried to the unmarked door between the two dressing rooms.

"Hello?"

No response.

Diana tried the handle and went in.

It was a storeroom of sorts, a dank and undecorated space containing various scaffolding oddments, metal frames and stacked cardboard boxes. Noah Dart sat on a solitary chair.

He looked at her, a surprised and distraught expression on his face.

"I'm sorry," she said. "Are you alright?"

He blinked. His gaze went to a laptop on the floor. The big crack along its case possibly explained the crashing she'd heard.

"You shouted," she said. "I thought someone was hurt."

He stared blankly then put his head in his hands and sighed. "The one thing we're never good at, us Brits. Expressing our emotions appropriately." He tried to laugh. "Is smashing up a perfectly good laptop an accepted part of the grieving process? Somewhere between denial and acceptance?"

Diana felt her panic subside. "Anger. Straight after denial and just before bargaining."

"I think I've already done that one." He nodded. "This thought, this idea, the loss of something – someone – so very very important... It's utter torment."

"You and Todd were old friends."

He pulled in a deep breath. "Him, me and our mate, Mitch. Student princes of song and dance. Like the three musketeers. Pathos, Athos and... Tinky Winky, whatever. Very much a partnership." He looked up at her. "Can I confess something?"

"Please do," Diana said.

"I don't think I'm angry that Todd's dead. There. Shocking, isn't it? I mean, I am sad about it but... Todd, Mitch and me. Old friends. Mitch was lost to an undiagnosed heart condition nearly twenty years ago. Now Todd. I think I might be angry because I can see it's my turn next."

Diana held in a laugh. Noah was only in his early fifties, a long way from death's door.

"Death makes us question our own mortality," she said. "That's normal."

"But also," he replied, "if I'm honest, I think I might be more emotional about what this means for the show. That's callous, right?"

"Not at all. I bet that at half the funerals out there,

there's someone with their mind on how they're going to pay the bills."

Noah nodded. A tear trickled down his cheek.

"The dead are dead," Diana said. "Grief and funerals and all that, that's for those of us who are left behind." She remembered something. "I thought you were going to be with Serena and the rest of the Americans at the hotel. The video call?"

He gave a dismissive wave. "I wasn't needed. This business has given them the excuse they needed to pull out of the deal." He sighed. "Another musical deal gone wrong for Noah Dart. But I'm just the guy who writes the songs, right?"

Diana nodded. "It's OK if you need to talk to someone about what you're going through. Either that or you'll need to buy more laptops to use as emotional punchbags."

Noah smiled and picked up the broken computer. "You're a wise woman."

"It's been said before," Diana replied.

Chapter Twenty-Seven

Zaf put another packet of biscuits into the basket. "What else looks fancy in here?"

Brie had a whole florentine between her teeth, which gave her a fierce, slightly manic look. "It's all fancy. Everything!"

"Cheese is good." He pointed at a huge display. "Everyone likes cheese."

"Mice like cheese."

"They do! It looks like Stilton is a big seller in here. Why's it packed in these weird urn things, though?"

"Urn," said Brie, as though tasting the word.

"I remember my aunt having something like that on her mantelpiece. She always said it was her dad. Now I realise it was cheese." Zaf shook his head in sorrow.

"Great Uncle Cheese," said Brie. "Shall we get some?"

"Yes, Brie."

Brie paused, her hand halfway to a pot of Stilton. "I thought we were getting Stilton?"

"We are."

"You said to get Brie."

"No. Brie is your name."

"It is. It is my name."

"What's Brie short for anyway?"

Brie looked down at herself. "Bad genes?"

Zaf frowned, not understanding. "Let's get some Stilton, Brie," he said in a silly voice.

They got two pots of Stilton: one to taste and one for the hamper.

A huge and colourful display caught Zaf's attention.

"They've got pickles. At least, I think it's pickles. Haven't these people heard of Branston?" He ran his hand across the jars. "It's like the Branston machine had a brain fart and made all these rogue pickles."

"Rogue pickles!" said Brie. "We should get one of each."

"There's so many. Rose petal chutney, fig and fennel chutney, asparagus piccalilli. Some of them sound a bit mad if I'm honest."

"I want to try that one," said Brie.

"Which one?"

"All of them. Get me a spoon. Let's find something to put on a sandwich, I'm starving."

"There's a deli," said Zaf. "I bet they do nice bread and then we could get some ham or something." He felt his stomach rumble. "I could really go for a ham sandwich with some chutney."

They found a loaf of bread. "Sourdough," said Zaf. "Should we get one for the hamper as well? It might go mouldy if the hamper's not going to Todd's family straight away."

"The sandwiches are just for us," said Brie. "Ooh, ham!"

"That's never ham. It looks like a prop from a zombie movie."

"Fancy ham looks like that." Brie dragged him towards a ham joint resting on a stand. "It's called CO-VAP... COVAP... COVAP..."

"COVAP Iberico."

"You *do* know all the languages." She waved at an assistant. "Some of the ham, please."

The assistant smiled. "How much would you like?"

"Uh, I dunno. A pound, maybe?"

Zaf shrugged his shoulders, unsure.

"Four hundred grams," said the assistant.

They both watched as he sliced the ham.

"It's quite a big pile, that," said Zaf.

"We need to taste a lot of chutney," Brie said.

They put the ham into their basket when it was

wrapped. As they walked away, Brie turned to Zaf. "Sandwich time."

"Time of the sandwiches."

They tore open the packet and each pulled out a piece of ham. Zaf realised he'd pulled out several, so he squeezed them together to fit in his mouth.

"Umf. Tasty."

The ham was chewy, but in a good way. He could see that it had hit the spot for Brie as well. They chewed in reverential silence for a few minutes.

"That is *really* good," said Brie.

"Be nice on a pizza, this."

"Mmm."

"I'm having some more."

"What's that?" Brie said to Zaf pointing behind him.

Zaf whirled around, adopting the defensive pose of a superhero, just in case.

"Uh oh. This looks like trouble, get behind me, Brie."

A small part of Zaf's brain knew that they were taking liberties by eating so much as they ambled round the store. In Asda, if you wanted to nibble the end of a French stick while you pushed your trolley round, that was fine as long as you paid for it. Was it the same in an upscale shop like Fortnum and Mason?

The approach of the stern-looking man and woman that Brie had spotted suggested that it wasn't.

"Are they security?" Brie whispered.

Zaf tried to keep an eye on the security people at the same time as turning round to talk to Brie. He managed it by swivelling one eyeball in each direction. It made him feel a little bit queasy.

"They must be. I'm guessing they're under-cover though. No uniform."

But the pair were watching them. And they didn't look happy.

"We could try smiling at them," said Brie. "That way we would show them that we are harmless and they might back off?"

"Let's give them our best smiles. Totally natural. On three. One, two, three."

Zaf and Brie smiled at full wattage, but to Zaf's horror, the security people also smiled. Their smiles were full of cruel mockery.

Zaf whimpered with fright. "They're monsters. D'you see the way they're looking at us?"

"Yes." Brie's voice was small. "What do we do?"

The smiles had fallen from the faces of the two security guards. Zaf eyed their solemn, penetrating gazes and tried to order his thoughts. "If they are trying to intimidate us, what is it they want?"

"Ultra violence," said Brie. "I can see it in their eyes."

"I reckon I could take them," said Zaf. He wasn't sure where that thought came from; it wasn't his usual approach. "Look at them, they don't look all that capable to me."

"We could just back slowly away," said Brie.

"No! That's the obvious thing. The best defence is a good offence."

"So how do we do that?"

"We take a confident step forward, maintaining eye contact."

"Let's do it."

Zaf ignored the wobble in Brie's voice. "Come on then, go!"

They took a co-ordinated step forward. So did the security people. They were so much closer now.

Zaf thought he should address them.

He cleared his throat. "I'm sorry?"

"*Are* we sorry?" asked Brie.

"No, it's fine," hissed Zaf. "This is the English version of 'I'm sorry?' which really means, 'What's your problem?'"

"Oh? I see."

The security people offered no reply but Zaf thought he could see them conferring with each other.

"Another step forward? Let's strike while the iron's hot," said Zaf. "Go!"

The security people also stepped forward. They could almost reach out and touch them. Zaf realised that he and Brie could no longer talk without being overheard, but Brie tapped him on the shoulder. "Do they look familiar to you?" she asked, pointing at the security people.

Zaf peered more closely. The man was about his

age and was black like him, although perhaps a little hollow-eyed and scary. The woman wasn't so easy to see as she was standing behind the man, but she was about Brie's height.

"Oh no. Wait. I think I know what's happ—"

"Is that a mirror?" Brie said.

Zaf reached out and tapped the flat surface. His weird doppelganger did the same. "Ouch. The lighting in here has made me look quite strange."

"It's definitely the lighting." Brie stepped forward and stared at her own face. "Can't be anything else. Can it?"

Chapter Twenty-Eight

"Hamper," Brie said suddenly.

"It's pronounced hamster," Zaf replied.

Brie pointed. "Hamper."

There was a stand entirely dedicated to hampers.

Zaf read the sign, trying to shake off the confusion with the mirror. "You can choose the stuff you want in a hamper and they make it up for you."

"Like a wishing hamper."

"Hamster."

"That's what we want to do," Brie said.

Zaf pushed himself to his feet. He couldn't remember sitting down.

"Hamper lady," he said, "can you help us please?"

"Certainly."

Zaf watched the assistant pick out a hamper. He admired her lovely Edwardian-style waistcoat.

The hamper lady arranged the things they'd selected into a wicker hamper. She made some suggestions about including cake and prosecco too.

"Hamper lady, you have worked magic," said Zaf when the entire thing was filled and finished with pretty packing straw.

"This is dead posh," said Brie, stroking the hamper. "It's proper old-fashioned with leather straps."

"Glad you're happy with it," said the woman. She was speaking in a clear, slow voice as though Zaf and Brie were foreign or stupid. "Shall we settle your bill?"

"Hmmm?"

Zaf realised there was a tall man in a uniform as equally posh and the sales assistants but which, somehow, conveyed the notion that he was shop security.

"Shall I help you get to the till to pay for all this?" he suggested, in a tone that also suggested that he wasn't really offering them a choice.

The polite but firm security man helpfully escorted them to a payment till where the contents of the hamper and their pockets were rung up.

"That will be eight hundred and seventy pounds, please," said the assistant.

Zaf laughed. "How much?"

"Eight hundred and seventy pounds. Cash or card?"

Zaf laughed again but Brie was handing her a credit card. "Here you are."

The woman hesitated before running it through the machine. "You did hear the total?"

"We did," Brie replied.

The woman gave them a look which Zaf couldn't read. "I have to ask. Are you two high?"

"Five-foot eleven's about right," said Zaf. He frowned. "What?"

"Are you perhaps...?" The woman did an impersonation of smoking a joint.

"We would never," said Brie. She frowned, then turned to Zaf, her expression running swiftly from shock to worry and then anger. "Are we high, Zaf?"

Zaf shook his head. Then he remembered.

"The brownies..."

"Your home-made brownies."

"I didn't make them! I didn't drug you."

His heart racing, he turned to the shop assistant. "We might be a little bit high. Yes."

"I thought so."

"Were we that obvious?"

The woman tilted her head. "The slice of incredibly expensive ham and the open pickle jar in your pocket kind of gave it away."

Zaf looked down at his pickle-smeared jacket. "We liked the pickle."

"Yes. We're very proud of our products," said the woman as she ran the credit card.

Chapter Twenty-Nine

Zaf tried to inspect the receipt as they made their way back down Piccadilly towards the Delphinium. It wasn't easy to read while he carried the huge hamper.

"Eight hundred? You have that kind of money?"

"I have Serena's credit card. Eight hundred's spare change for her." She was waving her hand in front of her face. "If we're high, shouldn't I be seeing motion trails when I wave my hand?"

"I don't know. I don't think so. I'm not the professor of drugs." He watched her as they walked, which made walking in a straight line all the more difficult. "You're taking this really calmly, the whole being high on hash brownies thing."

"Am I?" said Brie. "I thought I was freaking out,

but maybe I'm just too chilled with all the cannabis I've just freakin' eaten."

"Weed also causes people to experience paranoia," said Zaf, "so..."

"Don't tell me that now!" she snapped. "I'm very suggestible at this moment. You tell me I'm gonna be paranoid, them I'm..." She grabbed his arm. "Listen, this better wear off before I see Serena. She thinks I'm annoying anyway. She'll like me a lot less if she thinks I'm high."

"We can power through it," said Zaf, shoving his fist forward as if he were shattering bricks with his bare knuckles. This was unwise at it caused him momentarily to lose his grip on the hamper. He caught it with what felt like cat-like reflexes. A horn beeped and he realised he was now in the road. He quickly got back on the pavement.

"We need to just steer clear of people until we've come down a bit," said Brie.

"Right." He took a deep breath, but that seemed to send a heady rush through his brain and he held onto the hamper tighter. He was seized with slight panic. "Or we need to practise acting normal."

"Yes. We can't let them realise we accidentally got high and ate the most expensive ham money can buy."

"What does normal look like and how do we practise it?" Zaf asked.

Brie made a thoughtful humming sound. "Talk about the weather? That's a very British thing, yeah?"

"Good call! We can't go wrong if we stick to the weather. So, the sky is blue, it's warm but not too hot, and there's a tiny flutter of a breeze. That's a good twenty-minute conversation for the average Brit."

They went up to the stage door, where the grim doorman stared at them.

"Oho, Farrell! What about this weather, then?" Zaf said. "On a day like this, I reckon we all wish we were doormen."

"You making fun of me?" Farrell asked.

Zaf gulped. "No."

"We've got a bereavement hamper," said Brie.

"A what?" said Farrell.

"A bereavement hamper."

"A bereavement hamster." Zaf nodded. "For Todd."

"For his family," said Brie.

"Is that a thing now?" Farrell lifted the lid of the hamper. "I knew his wife, back in the day. Fine looking woman."

"Er, OK," said Zaf, not sure if that was the kind of thing one should be saying about a woman shortly after the death of her ex-husband.

"Ah. Stilton, cos you knew he was from Leicestershire originally. I get it. I get it. Spanish Jamón cos they spent all their summers out in Malaga. Nice. It's like a memory box of food."

"Exactly," said Zaf, who had no idea. "Memory box of food."

"And the pickles?" said Farrell.

Brie made a number of noises before saying, "Didn't she always call him her little pickle?"

"I wouldn't know about that," said Farrell. "But, yeah, it's a sweet gesture. You want, Marina on reception can get that sent up to them."

"Thanks," said Brie and helped Zaf through the door with the hamper.

Chapter Thirty

Diana knew that the secret to being in a place where you didn't belong was to move confidently and with purpose. It also helped to carry a sheet of paper or a parcel.

Diana had neither. She had only her duck-headed umbrella, but she clutched it firmly as though it was of the utmost importance that she deliver it somewhere as quickly as possible.

She found a flight of stairs along the side of the half-lit auditorium and tried to work her way up to the upper reaches of the theatre, if only to get a better understanding of the spot from which Todd had fallen to his death.

Just as Zaf had described, an encircling top-level corridor formed a horseshoe around the stage and auditorium. At the far end, a window in a side door overlooked the gantries of walkways, girders and wires above the stage.

She tried the door handle. It turned, but she wasn't about to go through. Too precarious.

Far below, dancers pivoted in unison on the stage. Diana peered down at them, and then turned back.

Just as she was about to retreat, she spotted a silhouette at the side of the stage. It looked like a little sandbag, the kind she'd seen used to counterbalance pulleys on the stage.

Then the little sandbag lifted a paw, licked it and used it to wash behind his ears.

"Gus."

Diana smiled. Newton would be relieved.

She looked back through the door, pondering.

So, Todd Granger, acclaimed stage director and lynchpin to a deal that would see *The Cockney's Complaint* transfer from London's West End to Broadway in New York, had come up here in the middle of a party and, possibly high as a kite, stepped through this door and over the edge into oblivion.

"But what were you doing up here?" she whispered.

Todd had been in the technical booth. Zaf had seen his cocktail glass there, and had heard Noah talking to a woman about the director. Diana made her way there.

It sat at the very base of the horseshoe corridor, giving a clear view of the stage and the auditorium.

She slipped inside. Three people worked at the computers and mixing desks, all wearing headphones. One was counting through a series of light changes to coincide with the activities on stage.

The woman at the sound mixing desk looked round at Diana. "You lost?"

"I wondered if you could help me with a few questions."

The woman gave a little frown.

"Todd Granger," Diana said. "He was up here, shortly before he died."

"Haven't you already asked us these questions?"

The woman thought she was a police officer.

"Questions get repeated a lot," Diana said, not correcting her.

"Expecting a different answer?"

"Maybe hoping to glean additional insights."

The woman raised a finger, cued up a sequence on the computer in front of her and pressed play.

"Right. Then let me recap. Yes, he was up here. He wanted to check up on some video files he'd asked us to transfer to digital and send on. No, he's not usually up here. No, he doesn't have an office of any sort. Yes, he did seem out of sorts and a bit weird but I guess that's what happens when you do cocaine. Yes, I think he had his drink with him when he came in but, no, it wasn't here when we returned. Maybe catering took it." The woman gave a flicker of a smile. "That the stuff you wanted to know?"

"Video files, you say?"

A sigh. "As we've said several times."

"Cue forty-seven," said one of the woman's colleagues, in a loud voice clearly designed to tell Diana how busy they were. *Go away.*

"Video files of what?" Diana asked.

The sound woman shook her head. "Personal stuff, not work stuff. Now, have you finished or do I have to tell your boss out there that we can't continue under these circumstances?"

"Boss?"

Diana stepped towards the long window and saw, on the very back row of the upper circle, the generous figure of DCI Clint Sugarbrook.

"Ah," she said. "Yes, I'll go check in with him."

She retreated and made her way to the nearest public entrance into the auditorium.

DCI Sugarbrook was already looking at her. He beckoned for her to come over.

"Miss Diana Bakewell." He patted the seat next to him.

Sugarbrook's seat was a squeeze for him. The armrests barely contained his muscly breadth, and his treetrunk legs were folded up against the seat in front.

Diana stood in front of the seat beside him. It wasn't comfortable, angling herself so she didn't topple into a seat, but she didn't like being bossed around. "These theatres were built when the average person was much smaller," she said.

"Tell me something I don't know. What are you doing here?"

She smiled and gestured around her. "I'm looking for our missing cat."

"No, you're not."

"Oh?"

She took the seat two along from him.

"Chocolate raisin?" he asked, angling a cardboard box towards her.

"Don't mind if I do." She leaned across and took one. "Are you still investigating Todd Granger's death? Is this how it's done? Sitting at the back of a theatre and watching rehearsals?"

"It's surprising what you see if no one thinks you're watching. Look there."

Further down in the auditorium, two figures had appeared. One was carrying a small wicker hamper.

Chapter Thirty-One

Zaf was glad of the theatre's gloom. His mind was churning, refusing to settle on anything for more than a few seconds. And he felt sick.

"Let's find somewhere quiet to sit for a bit," he said.

"You still buzzing?" asked Brie.

He frowned. "I'm not sure if I feel stoned at all now."

"Or you're so stoned you don't even know it. Like you could be naked in public and not think anything's wrong."

A jolt of fear sliced through him. "I'm not naked, am I?"

He looked down, patting himself.

Not naked. Phew.

"See?" said Brie. "Out of it, but unaware."

"You gave me a right fright."

"I'm hungry," said Brie. "Do you still have any of the fancy food on you?"

He inspected his pockets: pickles and ham. In his bag there was bread and other supplies.

"We should go have our picnic in a quiet bit of the theatre," he said. "Food'll help soak it up. Make us seem normal."

"The dress circle." Brie pushed him towards the side of the auditorium.

He stumbled forwards, unsure what a dress circle was. He could hear someone shouting instructions, putting the dancers through their paces for the big scene at the end of the musical.

Brie pushed him out of a door and up some stairs. At last, they came out above the seats they'd just walked through, looking down on the stage. It made Zaf feel dizzy.

He slumped into a chair and opened his bag of supplies.

"How shall we do this?" said Brie. "We haven't got plates or anything."

"We've got our laps." Zaf looked down at his lap. He frowned, looking around. "Maybe if we sit on the floor we can spread everything out."

They shuffled further along to the aisle that ran down the centre of the seating area, and emptied the bag onto the carpeted floor. The carpet had pink swirls that made Zaf's head spin.

Zaf demonstrated his proposed technique, imagining himself as a TV chef. "So I will take a slice of bread in this hand, and hold it out like a plate while I one-handedly apply some ham and maybe a small scoop of Stilton, too. Now I want to put some chutney on top before I top with another slice of bread."

"How're you going to do that when we haven't got a spoon?" Brie asked.

"Can you take the lid off and tip some on for me?"

"Sure." She opened a jar. "This one's fig and fennel." She tipped it over Zaf's hand, but the chutney stayed where it was.

"Solid stuff. Give it a little tap," Zaf said.

Brie gently tapped the base of the jar.

Nothing.

She tipped it upside down. "Come on!"

She whacked it hard, again and again, shaking the jar up and down.

Zaf giggled. "What are you doi... Oh."

A huge dollop of fig and fennel chutney had landed in his hand.

Brie looked at him, her expression shifting between horror and amusement. "I'm so sorry."

"No problem."

Zaf reached for another slice of bread and topped off his sandwich. He bunched it up and took a bite.

A large blob of chutney squirted out of the other side and slid onto his sleeve.

He chewed. "You can really taste the fennel. And the fig."

"I wouldn't know what either of them taste like," said Brie. "I'll have that spare bit." She used a slice of bread to scoop the stray blob of chutney from Zaf's sleeve.

She joined him in chewing. "It's nice, this. I must get stoned more often."

Zaf nodded. "Diana bakes hash brownies."

A nod. "Lots of older people smoke weed."

"Do they?" Zaf was surprised. "But she seems so... normal. Regular uptight middle-class white woman."

"Middle-class? Really? Even I can hear the estuary English in her voice."

"You've not seen her flat," he said. "It's like proper posh. Huge. These high ceilings like they had in the old days. And all her stuff."

"Stuff?"

"It's like she's really got her life together. It's just her. No partner or kids or anything but she's got her head screwed on just right." He chewed some more, thinking about Diana. "She never gives me grief, except for when I eat her food and..."

He stared at Brie.

"Oh my God."

"What?" she said.

"We ate her hash brownies. She's... She'll be well angry at me."

Brie frowned. "You live with Diana?"

"It's not like that," he blurted. "I've not been in London very long and I can't afford rent for a tiny shoebox in the worst borough of London."

"Huh. Try living in New York."

He raised an eyebrow. "*You* look like you've got your life together. Big shot job—"

"Getting shouted at by a narcissistic theatre producer?"

"But the money..."

"Ain't all that. My parents worked constantly, but that doesn't mean we weren't poor. Dad always waiting for that big break that never came. Mum working every job to pay the bills. No trust fund for me. I'd love to be on the receiving end of the megabucks from this show."

"What was it Diana said the other day? *Cats* has made like four billion dollars worldwide or something."

She nodded. "*Lion King*. Eight billion."

"No. Really?"

"If you can write the next *Book of Mormon* or *Hamilton* then you're on a ticket to fame and fortune."

She gestured into the distance in front of them and below, where a right old Cockney knees-up seemed to be taking place on stage. If Cockney knees-ups came with a full orchestral accompaniment.

"Noah Dart went from writing this hit to writing that stinker that was supposed to be playing across the road," she said.

"The Dick Whittington musical?"

She nodded. "Oh, the thought of having a hit on both sides of the street. But fate is fickle. I want more pickle."

He grinned. "That rhymes."

Brie eyed Zaf's sloppy sandwich and the open jar of pickle. "I think I need a spoon."

"What about those little wooden things that you eat ice cream with?" he suggested. "It's a theatre. They're bound to have somewhere."

He stood up, still eating. He set off in search of tiny ice cream spoons and at the end of the row almost walked straight into Newton Crombie.

The bus driver stepped back in surprise. "Zaf, are you looking for Gus too?"

"Newton! No. I've got pickle on me. I need a tiny spoon."

"You do," said Newton, looking down at Zaf's jacket.

"I'll help you look in a minute, though," said Zaf. "Brie and me got some snacks from our shopping trip."

Zaf showed Newton back to where they'd laid out all the food. "Newton's joining us."

Brie gave Newton a huge smile. "Very nice weather, Newton. I expect you noticed that the skies are blue, and the temperature is not too hot and not too cold."

"Er, yeah. Sure," said Newton. He looked sideways at Zaf and muttered, *"What's wrong with her?"*

"Newton, try the ham," said Zaf. "It's amazing."

Newton narrowed his eyes. "Wasn't this all supposed to go in the hamper?"

"There was the stuff we got for the hamper and the stuff we got to test," Brie explained.

Zaf was puzzled. "Where's the ham? Have you got it, Brie?"

She pointed. "It was right there, by the bread," said Brie pointing.

Newton crouched over the bread. He gasped. "Look!"

Zaf looked towards where Newton was pointing.

Right in the centre of the top slice of bread was a cat's paw print.

"Gus!" Newton cried, looking around.

"That explains where our ham went," said Zaf. Lucky cat: that was expensive ham.

"He was here!" Newton shouted. "Gus! Gus!" He hurried among the seats.

The voice on the stage stopped shouting at the dancers and bellowed "Silence!" out into the auditorium.

Newton ignored it, racing along the seats. He pulled at them, pushing down the seats and letting them bounce up again.

At last he arrived back with Zaf and Brie, panting.

"He'll have gone somewhere to enjoy that ham," he said, his voice flat. "I need to come back with a can of tuna or something."

"Aw, mate, I'm sorry," said Zaf. "We'll find him. Now, how d'you feel about Stilton? This stuff's gonna blow your mind."

Chapter Thirty-Two

"Did you see where the cat went?" asked Diana, leaning forward. They were at the very top of the upper circle and she had to crane her neck to see down into the front rows of the dress circle.

"That way." DCI Sugarbrook gestured off to the left. He surveyed Zaf, Newton and Brie below them. "Is that normal behaviour, for those three?" he asked.

Diana cocked her head. "Newton... well, he's more than a little attached to Gus. I can't really blame him. And as for Zaf and Brie..."

Truth was, she'd been trying to work out what they were up to. A picnic, in the theatre?

"Giggling like fools," said Sugarbrook. "Furtive like young lovers. Although unless I'm mistaken, your young colleague isn't into girls, is he?"

"I'm not sure what that has to do with you solving Todd Granger's murder."

He eyed her. "You're saying it was murder."

Diana rolled her eyes. "I don't think you'd be here if you didn't think that."

"Fair enough."

Diana gave Sugarbrook a sidelong glance. In the reflected light from the stage, his face was cast into sharp relief. He reminded her of one of the stone heads from Easter Island.

"What are you gaining from just sitting here, though?" she asked. "Where are the teams of officers combing the area? Where are the forensics people?"

Sugarbrook grunted. He popped another chocolate raisin in his mouth.

"I'm telling you nothing you don't already know," he said. "Todd Granger fell from the lighting rigs, his body full of cocaine. Pathologist's first suggestion, which we expect to have confirmed very soon, is that it was ingested, probably in the fruity drink several people saw him enjoying at the reception party."

Diana nodded: nothing she didn't already know, indeed.

The DCI gestured down towards the stage, where the buffet had been laid out on Monday. Right now it was filled with cavorting cockneys in flat caps.

"We've spoken to catering staff," he said, "and no one can say they saw Todd pick up that drink or who might have got it for him. There are cameras in here for filming live performances, but they weren't on. There's no CCTV and no useful footage from anyone's phone."

"It's a bit of a mystery," Diana said. "The fact that it was cocaine in his drink..."

"That doesn't help much." Sugarbrook sighed. "Without wishing to stereotype an entire industry, I can safely say there a number of people working in this space who either use or could access a quantity of nose toot powder. So, we have no forensic evidence and no strong material leads."

"But there are people and motives..."

"Too many to count." He looked at her with a frown. "And that's just the ones I know about. Even before considering spurned lovers or professional jealousies, I've got people practically falling over each other to present credible motives."

His chair creaked as he pointed down towards the stage.

Diana followed his gaze, allowing her eyes to adjust to the light. Charlotte Webber stood in front of the stage, huddled in conversation with Reuben Romano.

"The theatre manager and the American accountant had never met before this week," said Sugarbrook. "And now how would you describe them?"

"As thick as thieves," Diana said.

A nod. "I don't understand entertainment, but even I can tell neither of them wants to see this American deal go any further."

"But for Charlotte, that was about not wanting to lose her director or her leading man. You don't keep a man by killing him."

"His *death* might be accidental. Maybe the poisoning had a different intended outcome. But, yes, our leading man. Our Jack Ha'penny. He's a weirdly self-important little man."

Diana considered Gareth Booncastle. "He's an actor."

"He's got motives."

"The Hollywood film deal."

Sugarbrook frowned at her. "You *do* know more than you let on."

"I'm…" Diana breathed in. "I'm interested in people."

"Nosey?"

"No." She blinked. "Yes, I am nosey, but that's not what I meant. I'm interested in people. Their lives, their hopes, their needs. People get the wrong impression of London and Londoners. They say we're rude. They see how people don't meet each other's eye on the tube and assume every Londoner locks themselves away in their own little bubble just to get through the day. It's not true."

"Isn't it?"

She shook her head. "You watch Londoners. By and large, they survive on a hundred little interactions every day. Oh, they're as selfish and distracted as anyone else but the average Londoner is acutely aware of all the people around them. That's me."

"Acutely aware."

"My job is to help people, either to learn or to enjoy themselves. I do the tour guide work because I love people."

She looked at the spot on the stage where Todd had died, her chest dipping.

"Todd Granger's death was an upset, both an emotional upset to people who loved him, and an upset to the order of things."

"And you want to put it right," said Sugarbrook.

She heard the undertone in his voice. "I want to see it put right. But that's your job, isn't it?"

He raised an eyebrow. "This could go to coroner's inquest. It could come back as Death by Misadventure. The overdose could be judged to be self-inflicted."

"Is that what you think it is?"

"A verdict like that would restore order. It would let people get on with their lives. Most people would be happy with that."

"Even if it's not true."

He sighed. "There's very little more for us to go on right now. Our officers' time could be better spent elsewhere."

"And yet you're here," Diana said.

There was a hint of smile at the corner of his mouth. "I like the theatre. I like musicals. Who's to say

I can't spend an afternoon watching a hit West End show for free?"

"You don't strike me as the musicals type."

"Oh, me and my girls love a good musical."

"And is it? A good musical?"

He narrowed his eyes. "The story is simplistic enough. The late Victorian era, industrialisation eroding the old skilled professions. And we've got Jack Ha'penny, fruit seller and aspiring artist. Gareth Booncastle does a decent enough cockney by the way, especially for some plummy-voiced public school bloke. He finds a box of paintings belonging to a dead bloke, the father of the woman he's sweet on. He sells them and uses the money to help those who need it. There's the usual mistaken identity and misunderstandings between lovers, but it's all put right by the end of act two."

"I see."

"Do you?" said Sugarbrook. "One of the things I like about musicals is that everyone says what they're thinking. Well, sings it. No subtext. And by the end, everything is put right."

"In a way that rarely happens in the real world."

"Indeed," agreed the detective. "The real world's full of unsolved cases and unresolved grievances."

He turned to look at her. She was convinced the seat was about to break under his bulk.

"We may be able to find justice here for Todd Granger," he said. "We may not. But I can tell you none of it'll be helped by the interference of a nosey tour guide from Pimlico."

Diana opened her mouth to speak. She got the message, but *interference? Nosey?*

She'd admitted it herself, she supposed.

A raised voice came from down by the stage, causing her to lose her train of thought.

She turned to Serena McNash, with a small entourage of American visitors.

Serena was making some kind of announcement.

Chapter Thirty-Three

From up in the auditorium, Zaf could hear Serena addressing the theatre people.

"I have fantastic news, everyone."

Silence. Serena was waiting to be sure she had the full attention of everyone on the stage and in front of it.

Zaf leaned forwards, craning his neck. Brie stood up, her face tightening.

"The deal is going ahead," Serena said. "Despite the... unfortunate events of the last few days. You'll all be pleased to hear that the waters have been smoothed over and any ruffled feathers have been unruffled. Folks, the show must go on!"

There was scattered applause, led by the stage actors.

"I didn't realise the deal was really in doubt," he said.

"Nothing's ever certain till it's done," replied Brie, brushing food crumbs off herself.

"You going to be OK to face her?" he asked.

Brie patted herself down, squinting. "I'll be fine."

Zaf looked down at himself.

"You're a mess," Brie told him.

He inspected his food-smeared and grubby tour guide blazer and was forced to agree. He was, indeed, a mess. He slipped it off, then picked up the hamper and followed Brie to the exit as she headed for the stalls and her boss.

"At least Serena's in a good mood," he said as they descended the stairs from the dress circle.

"Trust me," Brie replied. "She can be at her most vindictive when she's happy."

They re-entered the auditorium. Serena was in front of the stage still, in conversation with Charlotte. She broke away as she spotted Gareth Booncastle walking across the stage.

Serena looked at Brie, then at the hamper. "Why didn't you have it sent straight over to the family?"

"I wanted to show you what we'd bought."

"The little girl has come to tell me she's been good at school today. Did you want a gold star sticker?"

"I was just—"

"Wasting time. I had other jobs for you today, Brie."

"I didn't know where you wanted it to go."

Zaf watched, aware that his mouth was hanging open. Serena had given him all those tips. Why did she see his worth but not Brie's?

"Serena, I hope you don't mind me saying," he said, "but I've been with Brie and she's worked really hard on this errand. Just like she works really hard on everything for you. Why don't you show her some appreciation?"

Serena gave Zaf the frostiest glare he'd had in some time. And he'd had practice, after eating Diana's chocolate mousse the previous week.

"Who the hell do you think you are," she said, "trying to tell me how to run my business? You think it's appropriate to criticise my people management in front of my employees? I've half a mind to call your manager right now."

Zaf knew he'd crossed a line. But he also knew Serena was a bully.

He had to keep his job safe, regardless of what he thought of her. She was a client.

"I'm sorry you feel that way," was all he could squeeze out.

He backed away swiftly, his cheeks hot. He hurried up the auditorium steps and found Diana waiting for him, his blazer draped over her arm.

"Are you alright?" she said.

"I've made Serena angry." He resisted the urge to turn and look.

"You?"

"I kind of overstepped the mark. I thought that since she'd been tipping me heavily…"

"Ah." Diana nodded. "Thought it bought you the right to get a bit familiar with her?"

He nodded.

Diana tilted her head: *let's head out.* They had no more professional commitments today.

"Tipping is a funny thing," said Diana as they walked out of the theatre onto Coventry Street. "A lot of it is unconscious or automatic, driven by politeness or guilt. Sometimes by genuine gratitude."

Zaf squeezed past a group of tourists looking up at the sparkling theatre signage above their heads. "I thought she liked me."

Diana chuckled. "For some people, tipping establishes power. *I tip you because I'm better than you, and by tipping you, I demonstrate that I own you.*"

"Wow. I guess."

They stopped at a pedestrian crossing, Zaf looking around at the excited theatregoers. For him it was the end of a work day, but for these people it was the beginning of a magical evening in a darkened theatre.

"Which also leads," Diana said, "to the weird scenario where some people refuse to tip out of a perverse respect for the service provider."

"I've seen that."

"Our Serena McNash back there. I suspect she's

definitely got a mistress-and-servant Downton Abbey relationship in her mind when she tips you. She certainly didn't want you turning into an uppity little manservant."

Zaf sighed. It had been an emotional rollercoaster of a day.

Being roasted by Serena had shaken him more than he liked to admit. He felt guilty about spending all that money on ham, and about letting Gus the cat steal it. And on top of all that, his stomach was complaining about all the weird food.

He patted his growling belly, wondering if it was the cannabis brownies, the half-jar of pickle, or the strangely moreish Stilton.

The walk home was slow; he felt heavy and his indigestion made him sluggish. And the fact that Diana would spot the missing brownies when they got home was nagging at him.

More than once, Diana had to stop and check he was fit to walk. He was tempted to catch a bus but didn't want her to know how much he'd eaten.

At last, they arrived at the flat. Zaf went to his room to change out of his work clothes and remove the final scraps of food from his pockets.

As he shut himself in the bathroom to scrub the pickle stains off his clothes, he heard Diana's voice from the kitchen.

"Zaf!"

He held his breath.

Diana didn't shout. Not like that, anyway.

"Zaf!"

He sighed and opened the bathroom door. "Yes?"

"Come here."

Chapter Thirty-Four

Diana was standing by the open fridge, staring at Zaf as he entered the kitchen.

"Where are the brownies, Zaf?"

"OK." He raised his hands for calm. "In my defence, two things. First, I didn't know you were the hash brownie kind of woman, and I had no idea that—"

"Where are the brownies, Zaf?"

"And... and there was definitely a note that said *eat these* or something like it."

"You took that as an instruction."

She broke open a brownie from the untouched box and sniffed.

"Those were special brownies, Zaf."

"I know. *Now* I know. I didn't at the time. I needed a snack and maybe I didn't read the note in the way you meant—"

"Where are they?"

"We ate them."

"*We?*"

"Brie and me. In my defence—"

"Stop saying *in my defence!*"

"Hey!" he said, feeling his own anger rise and regretting it instantly. "We didn't know, right? And if it makes you feel any better, I've felt sick for most the day."

Diana shook her head. "There were loads in there! What possessed you?"

Zaf shrugged. "I was in a rush. I had no idea... they were strong... I've had to work so hard to hold myself together. Honestly, the day I've had today it's a miracle I even survived."

"What do you mean?"

Zaf couldn't explain. An over-indulgence of luxury food didn't sound like the worst day, after all.

He shrugged. "Just, you know." He held up his dirty blazer like that might explain.

It didn't.

"You're lost for words?" she said. "Any other time you can talk for Britain. Which is probably just as bad."

"What's that supposed to mean?"

"You're impulsive," Diana said. "You say the first thing that flits into your head, just like you eat any food that you come across. Sometimes it would be nice if you stopped to think."

"Maybe I like to be true to myself."

"What?"

"It's called being authentic, Diana. You're the one who's always going on about it."

"There's a difference between being authentic and having no filter. Sometimes we have to think about what we do and say for the sake of others."

He glared at her. "Says the person who daubed herself with my most expensive cosmetics."

Her jaw was clenched. "I haven't touched your things since you mentioned it. I noticed the pile of soap you stole from the gift bags on Monday, which was either a sweet gesture or a less than subtle dig. But I've not touched your products."

"Well, I think the damage has been done there."

"You want me to pay you back for what I've used?" she said. "And should I start charging you rent?"

Zaf felt his chest hollow out. "You know money's tight."

"You've still got enough to go out clubbing at night. Don't think I don't hear you creeping back in at three in the morning. You're no silent ninja, Zaf. Far from it."

"Oh, now you're clocking me in and out, huh? Maybe I need to go out to get some space sometimes. Maybe I need to escape, particularly when I don't know what'll annoy you next. It's like walking on those things... oh, those things you have to walk on when you don't know how people are going to react."

"Eggshells." Diana's arms were folded across her chest.

"Thank you," he snapped. "You don't even tell me you're annoyed until you're ready to boil over. I can't listen if you don't say anything."

"Maybe I shouldn't have to tell you."

"I'm not a mind-reader. I'm a man. I don't have female intuition."

"I think the quality you're referring to is basic human empathy, Zaf."

He stared at her. There was a nasty taste in his mouth, and it wasn't from the picnic.

"You..." He took a breath. "You've been kind to let me stay here, Diana, but it's not working. I'll pack a bag and move out tonight."

She nodded, slowly and sadly.

Zaf's phone buzzed in his pocket.

"What is it now?" he snapped. This wasn't the time.

He grabbed it: Brie Grebbson. She was calling him.

"Something's wrong," he said.

"How do you know?" said Diana.

"No one under the age of thirty phones unless it's an emergency."

He clicked to answer. "Yes?"

"Zaf? Zaf?" Brie panted.

"Brie. Is everything OK?"

"You need to tell me if I'm still tripping, Zaf."

Zaf turned away from Diana's frown. Was that concern, or disapproval?

"I'm sure you're fine," he said into the phone.

"But I'm not. I thought I was imagining it, the drawers and the cupboard aren't lined up. My clothes, they've been moved."

"What are you talking about?"

"Either it's the paranoia kicking in or, um... Zaf, I think someone's broken into my room."

"Broken into your room?" He ran a hand over his short hair. "Brie, I don't..."

"I'm scared, Zaf. Has someone..."

Zaf swallowed, searching for words to reassure her.

Brie had eaten enough food to fell a horse. And as for the brownies...

She had to be imagining it.

"Come on," Diana said behind him.

He turned to see her grabbing her brolly from its place on the back of the dining chair.

"Zaf?" said Brie.

"Hang on." He gave Diana a questioning look.

"We're going to the Redhouse Hotel," she said.

"Seriously." Zaf put his hand over the phone's microphone. "Brie's probably still a bit high. It's nothing."

"Zaf?" Brie's voice was muffled.

"If that's the case, at least the trip out will do us good," said Diana, not meeting his eye.

Zaf clenched his jaw. "Hold tight, Brie. We're coming over."

Chapter Thirty-Five

Diana had been right to insist they left the flat. The irritation that had been simmering inside her dissipated as the number 13 bus took them further away from the flat. Zaf's body language seemed to relax, too. As they passed Hyde Park Corner, he even pointed out some street performers doing a dance that he knew would make her laugh.

She laughed along with him. She even made eye contact with him.

Sure, Zaf could be annoying. And yes, Diana wasn't a fan of communal living. But he was her colleague, and he needed her help.

Still. This couldn't be a long-term arrangement.

They arrived at the Redhouse Hotel twenty minutes later to find Penny still at the reception desk. Diana raised her brolly in greeting.

"Can't you stay away?" Penny asked, smiling.

"We're just popping up to see a guest," Diana replied. "Can you call up to her?"

"Room one-three-two," said Zaf, already hurrying towards the stairs.

"One-three-two then," Diana repeated, following him.

Zaf started up the stairs, two at a time.

Diana watched him. She was fit for her age, but she wasn't about to start running up stairs.

By the time she reached the first floor, Zaf was at the open door of Brie's room, talking to the young woman.

"You didn't both need to come," Brie said. "I mean I'm grateful but..."

Diana arrived at the doorway. "I thought I'd see where the other half of my brownies went."

Brie's cheeks reddened.

"How are you feeling?" Diana asked.

"I think I've got myself into a bit of a panic." Brie's shoulders slumped. She looked between Zaf and Diana then turned into her room. They followed.

Diana surveyed the room. For one that had supposedly been broken into, it was remarkably ordinary.

The bed was tidy. A large suitcase sat on the suitcase stand by the window, open and empty. The wardrobe doors were closed and there were few belongings on the surfaces.

Diana smiled. "You keep the place tidy."

Brie looked around. "I may have done a little tidying when I heard you were coming over."

"And have you told anyone else that you think you've had a break-in?"

Brie gave her a helpless look. "It's been a weird day. I didn't want to add to the weirdness. I'm very much the junior member of the tour trip."

"And telling your colleagues about this might be seen as weakness."

"Exactly."

"We're over-reacting," said Zaf. "I'm sure it's all fine."

Diana wasn't so sure.

She knelt by the drawer unit underneath the wall-mounted TV. There were deep indents in the carpet, a full inch away from where the unit's feet now stood.

"Have you moved this?" she asked.

"No," replied Brie.

"You think someone's been moving your furniture?"

"It might have been housekeeping."

Diana turned to look up at Brie. "But...?"

"They've never moved it before." Brie walked towards the chest of drawers next to the bed. "And I'm sure my drawers aren't how I left them."

"Is anything missing?" said Zaf.

Brie shook her head. "Cards, passport, phone, laptop. Nothing missing."

Diana turned a full circle, slowly inspecting the room. "If you've had burglars, they're the neatest burglars I know."

Zaf gave her a look: *you know a lot of burglars?* She ignored it.

"That's what makes it creepy," Brie said. "If I knew I'd had a break in then I could do something. But this... Do you think someone's been here? You came over here damned quick."

"We needed to stretch our legs," said Diana.

She'd wanted to get out of the flat. But more accurately, she'd been intrigued.

Had Clint Sugarbrook been right when he'd described her as *nosey?*

She was concerned about her guests. She didn't like the way Todd Granger's death had affected the group.

And yes, she had to admit it. She was nosey.

There was a mystery here. Diana couldn't stand *not knowing* things.

She went back to the door. There was no sign of forced entry.

"I'll go have a quick chat with reception."

She left Zaf with Brie and headed back down to the lobby, taking the lift this time. As she walked she scanned the corridor, the ceiling, the other doors.

Downstairs, she passed the restaurant on her way from the lift to the reception desk. Serena McNash was in there, sitting alone at a candle-lit booth. The woman looked tired, her face downcast.

Penny was still at reception, her expression puzzled and not a little worried. "Is everything OK?"

Diana considered. "Can I tell you something without it suddenly becoming all official?"

"That sounds ominous."

Diana stepped closer to the desk, lowering her voice. "Someone has been in one of our guests' rooms."

"Someone," said Penny. "As in...?"

"Moving furniture. Rifling through her things."

"Are you making an accusation—"

"I'm not making anything, Penny. I think there's something going on among our American visitors and I wondered who might have access to that room."

"One-three-two." Penny typed on the computer. "The keycard was used a couple of times before nine a.m. Then twice, at ten fifteen and ten twenty-five. That was probably housekeeping. And then not again until just before six. That was your guest returning, I guess."

"So, in the time Miss Grebbson was out, only housekeeping went in?"

"I could ask Carmen if you like, the cleaner assigned to that room. She's still in the building."

"Oh, I wouldn't want to make a fuss..."

Penny shook her head. "I'll call her."

A couple of minutes later, a short woman approached from the stairs. Penny beckoned her over.

"Carmen," she said. "This is Diana Bakewell, from Chartwell and Crouch."

Carmen gave Diana a nod and a tight smile.

"She's just come from room one-three-two," Penny continued, her voice little more than a murmur. "She's wondering why the unit under the TV's been moved."

"I have not moved any furniture," Carmen replied in a clipped southern European accent. "I am not expected to move furniture."

"No," said Penny.

"You went into the room twice," Diana said.

"I emptied the vacuum cleaner," said the maid. "It was making a noise. When I came back, the man of the room came in with me."

"The *man* of the room?" Diana exchanged a glance with Penny.

Penny's shoulders sagged. "I can call the police."

Diana waved the notion away. "Nothing appears to be stolen. Also, I've got a feeling this isn't an outsider." She turned to the maid. "Carmen. The man who came to the room. Was he English? American?"

Carmen shrugged. "I thought it was his room."

"I can show you some photos." She'd need to speak to Zaf. He was still up there with Brie, Diana assumed.

"Are you sure?" said Penny.

"Will you get into trouble if you don't call the police?" Diana asked her.

Penny sighed. "Hotel policy is one thing. My manager, Carlton, wouldn't want to disturb the police or upset other guests by causing a scene."

"Ah, managers," said Diana. "A law unto themselves." She tapped her fingers on the desk and walked back towards the lifts.

Chapter Thirty-Six

Diana headed back to the lifts, glancing into the restaurant and spotting Serena, still alone, with a whiskey tumbler cradled in her hands.

The producer looked up and their eyes locked for a long moment.

Diana sighed: she couldn't walk on, not now.

She turned into the restaurant.

"I know I'm not one of the theatre people," she said, but I wanted to offer my congratulations for the deal. Well done on getting it all signed."

Serena nodded. "Agreed, not signed. But the finishing post is just a hair's breadth away." She rolled the tumbler from one palm to the other. "My body clock is shot to hell. I think it's... What time is it?"

Diana checked her watch. "Nearly seven p.m."

Serena nodded. "My body thinks it's lunchtime."

"Whiskey o'clock?"

Serena gave a hard laugh. "It's not been a good week. Sit. If you have time…"

"I do."

A waiter approached.

"A John Collins please," Diana said. She tapped out a message to Zaf as she slid into the seat next to Serena, asking him to send her any photos he had of the tour group.

"You don't strike me as a cocktail drinker," said Serena.

"What *do* I strike you as?" asked Diana, curious.

"A cup of tea in a china cup with a little English scone on the side."

Diana laughed. "I'm that too. Never underestimate the power of a decent cup of tea."

"I like London," Serena said.

"I'm glad."

"I've been here more than a dozen times in the last twenty years. There's something intrinsically fascinating about the British theatre system, the British attitude to theatre. I guess you've had a few hundred years more practice at it than us."

"Shakespeare's Globe isn't far away, across the river in Southwark. It's worth a visit."

Serena shrugged. "There's something special in the air here. The land that gave us Shakespeare."

"I don't know about that," said Diana. "Many

would say Shakespeare simply stole other people's plots to create his best-loved plays."

"All art is plagiarism, my dear. It's the construction that counts."

The waiter arrived with Diana's drink. The gin cocktail had been topped with a complex fold of lemon rind, skewered with a long plastic pin.

"A man called John Collins, who worked in a bar in Conduit Street in Mayfair..." Diana paused to get her bearings, then gestured southwards. "... some distance that way, is credited with inventing the Tom Collins cocktail."

"And *did* he?"

She shrugged. "Like so much London history, who created what depends on who you talk to. Maybe it was no one at all." She smiled, remembering something. "In the eighteen seventies, there was a popular hoax in New York which revolved around telling people Tom Collins was looking for them or had been talking about them in a bar."

"Your knowledge isn't limited to London, then?"

"London is my speciality." Diana sipped the drink. It was sharp and sweet on the tongue.

"You know," Serena said, "you have my accountant convinced he's gonna find evidence of his noble Roman ancestry here."

"It's all around us."

Serena smiled. She looked both tired and energised. Too awake to sleep, too tired to give in.

"That man is insufferable at times," she said. "Oh, he's a fine accountant, but I only brought him over here as a favour to my sister."

"Oh?"

Serena pushed out an exasperated breath. "He's my ex-brother-in-law. He and my sister divorced last year. But for a man good with contracts and the law, he seems to find it difficult to comprehend the notion that they are no longer together."

"You've whisked him across the ocean so he can forget his former love."

"Perhaps. Maybe open his eyes to the wider world and new opportunities. In that, at least, I think I've succeeded. But between that and Todd's death and everything else..."

Diana eyed her. "Your personal assistant, Brie—"

Serena's expression sharpened. "What about her?"

"She seems a smart cookie."

Serena pressed her lips together until they were almost white and bloodless.

"She is," she said, eventually. "But she is guilty of twin crimes I don't think I can forgive."

"Yes?"

"Competence and youth."

Diana laughed.

"I like to surround myself with competent staff," Serena said, "and I'm a big believer in giving young people experience in the theatre management business. But both of them in one body... Ugh. I look at her and I see her gunning for my job in five years' time. And she doesn't understand how much harder it was for women in the workplace a generation ago." She looked up from her drink. "You know what I mean."

Diana nodded. "In a former life, I worked in the music industry."

"Really?"

"I had a good voice."

"I heard... the other night in the pub."

Diana took a sip of her drink. "I loved every minute of it. Or at least, I remember loving every minute of it. But times were different then. It was a man's world."

"It's still a man's world. Can you picture all the people lining up to see this latest venture of mine fail? But, yeah, the Bries of this world have it easy by comparison. And yet..."

"And yet?"

Serena downed her drink. "Musical theatre has changed a lot in that time, too. Not always for the better."

"You think?"

"This business I'm in right now. It's about a commercialised commodity, and you guys started it."

"Us?"

"The musicals I fell in love with as a little girl... *Oklahoma, Cabaret, West Side Story.* They were the old school plays with songs. A theatre, a set, a story. All you needed was a stage."

"Some cracking tunes."

"Some of the best. But then along comes Mr Andrew Lloyd Webber and *Cats*."

"We were talking about it the other day."

"Sure, you love your cat. But that musical turned a straightforward stage production into some weird and magical commodity where the audience was totally immersed in a world of sound and action. Theatre not as performance but as experience, the same thing Cirque de Soleil did for circuses. A product, heavily merchandised, easily exportable."

"I never thought of it that way," said Diana.

"Suddenly, theatre isn't playing catch up with TV and film. It's leading the way. And London's West End is the hothouse where many of these shows are still conceived." Serena pushed her glass away. "That's the world we live in now. That's the sea Brie Grebbson is learning to swim in."

"And that's the reason you give Miss Grebbson something of a hard time."

Serena's expression cooled. "What would you know? You're just a London tour guide."

"Oh, yes," Diana agreed. "I am just a London tour guide."

Chapter Thirty-Seven

Zaf was waiting with Brie when he received Diana's text.

Send me photos of the tour group if you can, please.

Wondering why she needed them, he pulled up the snaps he'd taken over the last couple of days and sent them to her via WhatsApp.

What was she doing downstairs? Would she come back when she'd done whatever she needed the photos for?

At least the wait gave Brie enough time to get her head back together.

Prompted by Diana's message, he sat on the bed next to her and started showing Brie photos of London. She responded by pulling up photos of New York.

"You'd like it in New York," she said.

"I would," he replied.

"The winters are bitterly cruel, though."

Zaf tilted his head. "I've got my eye on a luscious faux-fur coat. It needs a bitter winter so I can showcase it."

There was a knock on the door. Brie's head jerked up.

He gave her what he hoped was a reassuring smile. "It's just Diana."

Brie nodded, checked the spy-hole, then opened it. He was right.

"Someone was in here," Diana said as she entered. "They lied to the maid."

Brie nodded. "What's going on? Either your tour company has amazing customer service, or you think there's something fishy going on."

Diana opened her mouth, lost for words. It wasn't often Zaf saw that happen.

"We *do* think there's something going on," he said. "The police reckon Todd's death is suspicious."

"What does this have to do with my break-in?"

Zaf looked at Diana. Again, she said nothing.

"Todd died in an unexpected way," he said, "during an important week for *The Cockney's Complaint*. I'm not sure how that's linked to your break-in, but it feels dodgy."

"Do you have any other connection to Todd?" Diana asked. "Anything that might be relevant?"

Brie sighed. "He knew my mum and dad years ago. They all worked in the theatre. But in the last ten years or so, I've had hardly any contact with him at all." She looked at Zaf. "A few social media likes, a Christmas card each year. Although we've both been working on the Broadway transfer of *Cockney* I don't think we've exchanged more than a few words. He's more..." She raised her hands in a shrug. "He's just a face in an old picture or an old family video. Todd Granger, director."

She swiped on her phone and held it out for them to see.

Zaf leaned in to see a low-resolution photograph of a party. A Christmas gathering, by the look of the jumpers.

Brie's finger ran along the line of people pictured. "Todd's wife Clarissa. Todd. Noah and a woman he was going out with at the time, I can't remember her name. There's my mum leaning on the piano."

Her finger shifted to a man sitting at the piano, a little girl in a yellow princess dress on his knee. "And that's my dad and me, in a no doubt highly flammable Beauty and the Beast dress."

She paused while they scanned the faces.

"That's who Todd was," she said, finally. "I think, after a while, that's who everyone becomes. A face in a photograph with a few memories kind of attached to it."

Diana nodded.

"Then there's no link between you and Todd," she said. "Not really."

Zaf exchanged sad smiles with Brie as Diana moved over to the dresser by the wall. She inspected the feet and then the top.

"But someone came in here," she said, "looking for something. If they moved furniture that suggests they were looking for something specific, unless they're the most thorough burglars I've ever come across."

Zaf wondered again if Diana had come across a lot of burglars.

Diana ran her fingers along the gap between the top of the dresser and the wall.

"It was a slim object," she said.

"Slim." Zaf nodded. Her fingers didn't fit into the gap.

Diana's gaze was on Brie's face. "A piece of paper. A note. A cheque. A credit card. A business card. A gold chain. A photograph."

Brie shook her head.

"I'm not missing anything. I've looked through my things."

"Charger cables," said Zaf. "I'm always forgetting my phone charger when I leave places. That and headphones."

"A burglar breaking in to steal charger cables?" asked Diana.

"I'm just saying that sometimes you don't know what you've lost until a while after."

"I'll double check," said Brie.

Diana sighed. "And on that note, it's probably time for us to go."

Zaf nodded and stood up. "Message any time if you need to."

"Thanks." Brie stood to hug him.

Diana and Zaf strolled out of the hotel. Night had fallen over the city now, but there was still the light and noise of traffic.

They walked south towards Oxford Street and Marble Arch. People thronged around them; tourists enjoying the warm evening, Londoners scurrying home or on their way to a night out.

"Will we ever know what happened?" said Zaf as they waited for the red man to turn green on the far side of Marble Arch. They'd got in the habit of crossing Park Lane to walk along the Hyde Park side. It was quieter, and the air felt less heavy.

"Oh, I hope so," Diana replied.

He eyed her; did she know more than she was letting on?

She turned and gave him a smile as the lights changed and they crossed the road. The crowds jostled them, then thinned out as they headed south past the park.

It wasn't until they'd stepped into the underpass under Wellington Arch at Hyde Park Corner that Zaf remembered their last conversation, before Brie had called about her break-in.

He'd said he was going to move out.

He swallowed. "I need to pack my things."

"It's late now," Diana replied with a thin smile. "We have work in the morning. Let's leave it for now."

She'd been quick with an answer; had she been thinking about it too?

"Are you sure?" he asked.

Diana said nothing, just walked on towards Victoria and the flat beyond.

Chapter Thirty-Eight

The next morning, Diana received a message from Carolyn.

I've made arrangements with the Port of London Authority. Your group can come mudlarking at Greenwich.

She looked up to see Zaf entering the depot.

"Someone looks happy," he said.

"Just got the confirmation," she replied, waggling her phone. "We're going to be mudlarks for the day."

"Cool."

She pointed at his blazer. "I can still see that food stain."

"Really? I thought I'd washed it off."

"It's like a whole jar of chutney died on your blazer and left a ghostly imprint behind. Get one of the spares from the cupboard. When you've done that, can you go to the hotel? Tell all our guests to wear suitable footwear and gloves."

"What if they don't have them?"

Diana smiled. "I'm loading a bag of spares."

Zaf nodded and turned towards the cupboard. He paused.

"About last night..."

"Yes." Diana nodded. "I've been thinking about Brie's break-in too."

"No, not that. I mean us. The flat sharing thing. If you still want me to move out, I totally understand. I can—"

"Can we talk about this later, Zaf?" Diana was trying to sound neutral, but worried she'd come across as cold. "Let's get through this morning, yes?"

Newton walked towards the bus, a bulging carrier bag in his hand.

"Planning a picnic?" asked Diana.

"Tuna, dreamy-treats and Mr Squeaksalot."

"Mr Squeaksalot?"

The driver pulled out a ragged grey felt blob. "It's Gus's favourite toy. Today's the day I shall rescue him from the theatre."

Diana opened her mouth to offer encouragement, but was interrupted by Paul Kensington stalking out of his office. She closed her mouth, waiting to hear what insane ideas he was about to shower them with.

Paul Kensington was not a big man. While not exactly short, he somehow lacked any kind of presence or stature. With his short-sleeved shirts and little ties, he looked like he did all his shopping in the 'back to school' section of a supermarket.

Stalking didn't come easily to him, and the effect was more of a waddle.

"You're planning today's excursion, yes?" he demanded of Diana.

"I am."

"You have plans for the group that won't leave me with a huge bill or a lawsuit?"

Diana nodded. "We're going paddling in history."

Paul Kensington gave her a look that had become familiar: he had no idea what she was talking about, but he wanted to be sure she understood that he was in charge.

Diana often imagined him practising it in front of a mirror.

"Going to walk barefoot in the Princess Diana memorial fountain?" he suggested.

"No, something far more earthy than that. Don't worry, Paul. We have an excellent guide."

Newton started up the bus's engine. Diana gave Paul a cheery wave as she stepped on board and he frowned in response.

She shrugged and took a seat at the front of the bus. They headed out of the depot and down the road to collect their guests.

At the hotel, Diana hopped off and strode into the

reception. Zaf was already there, waiting for the American guests. Penny was behind the desk, chatting with Zaf.

Diana remembered something.

"There was a package for Brie on Monday," she said.

"Pardon?" said Penny.

"On the evening of Todd's death, you told Brie a package had been sent to her room."

"I did?" Penny frowned, remembering. "Monday. Yes. A package. Barely more than a card."

"A card," Diana repeated.

"It was from the theatre," Penny said. "I don't think there was a sender's name or anything on it."

Zaf gasped. "Todd's present!"

Diana gave him a quizzical look.

"I spoke to him at the drinks thing," Zaf said. "Um, what did he say? Er, there were hugs and he said she was knee-high to a grasshopper the last time he'd seen her and then he just said he had a gift for her. It would be later."

"You're right," she said. "I remember you telling me. So this card, that must have been the gift."

"Is this important?" asked Penny.

Diana chewed her lip. "Someone *did* go into Brie's room. They were willing to move furniture to look for it. They knew which room Brie was in."

"And they knew she'd be out," said Zaf.

Penny grunted. "Bereavement hamper."

"Pardon?" Diana said.

"A bereavement hamper. Have you heard of anything like that before?"

Diana realised what Penny was talking about. "Brie was given a task. The bereavement hamper. Maybe the point was to get her out of the hotel."

"It was Serena who asked her," said Zaf. If Serena ever *asked* Brie to do anything, he thought.

Diana considered this. "But the maid said the person in the room was a man."

"Reuben," said Zaf. "The accountant."

Penny leaned across the desk. "Are you suggesting the two of them killed Todd?" Her voice had dropped to a clandestine whisper.

"We're considering options," Diana said. "Definitely not making unfounded accusations."

Zaf cleared his throat and turned. Diana straightened to see members of the American delegation approaching down the corridor.

She surveyed them, checking they were dressed for the occasion. Most were, but Serena was wearing the same high heels she always had on.

Diana approached the producer. "Serena?" She glanced down at her shoes. "Do you have some more suitable footwear? Those won't work at all for today's activities."

"I have boots in the bag." Serena held up a tote bag. "I'm just wearing these for the journey."

"Right you are." Diana glanced at the bag, then at

Serena's trousers. They were a pale lemon colour. Maybe she could protect them from the mud by tucking them into her boots.

Reuben Romano had taken his attire more seriously. He wore protective nylon overtrousers tucked into boots, and had acquired yellow washing up gloves from somewhere. They stuck out of his shirt pocket like a handkerchief with rubber fingers that waved to passers-by.

"Very smart," Diana commented.

"We're delving into history," he said. "Finding evidence of my forebears."

Diana frowned. "Ah. Yes. The Romans."

"I've come well-prepared. Did you know that the oldest Roman item found in the city is a timber drain from forty-seven A.D?"

"Is it, indeed?"

"The original settlement ran along the Thames from the Tower of London to Ludgate Road."

"Ludgate Hill, yes."

"Are we going there?"

"We're not allowed there, sorry. We're going to Greenwich, a few miles to the east."

A downcast look swept across his thin face.

"The Romans would have been there too," Diana added. "Greenwich was a natural landing point on the river, then and now. Fishermen would have worked there. Soldiers would have come ashore there."

Her words perked him up. "Really?"

She nodded. "Really."

He gave her a satisfied smile and headed out to the bus.

Diana followed, leaving Zaf to wait for the final stragglers. As she emerged onto the pavement, she spotted Gareth Booncastle strolling down the road towards her.

Gareth seemed to have dressed for an upper-class pheasant shoot. He wore plus fours and tweed, and strode along the street as if he owned the place. It was an outfit that was both deeply appropriate and wildly inappropriate for wading in the muddy banks of the Thames.

Diana saw that he was limping, struggling to avoid putting too much weight on his right leg. His eye caught hers and he attempted to turn the limp into a shuffling, dancing, skipping walk. By the time he reached the bus, he was deliberately and clearly walking with no limp at all.

"Are you not performing tonight?" Serena asked him as he mounted the bus, her eyes narrowed in suspicion.

"Of course. But I couldn't miss the chance to spend one more day with you lovely people."

"Are you going to badger me about your contract again?"

"Wouldn't dream of it." He gave her a wide smile.

"The conversation's been had. All that can be said has been said, apparently. The time for words has passed."

The last of the passengers got on, Zaf bringing up the rear. Brie settled a few seats away from Serena and offered Diana a tired smile.

Chapter Thirty-Nine

Diana picked up the microphone as they looped around Great Cumberland Place. "The first sight on our trip today is just ahead: Marble Arch."

"All I can see is road signs and traffic lights," muttered Reuben.

Diana surveyed the arch, stranded in the middle of the road system. "It does look a bit out of place, doesn't it? Apparently it was originally built as an entrance to Buckingham Palace, but was moved to its present location when there was building work on the palace."

"And they never put it back?" Reuben asked.

"I heard it was too small for the state coach to pass through," said Brie.

"I've heard that story too," said Zaf, "although apparently the state coach has been through it. But Brie's version is more interesting."

He shared a smile with the young woman. She still looked tired, and turned to gaze out of the window, her chin slumped on her folded arms.

They rumbled through the traffic lights and everyone turned to look at the arch. The traffic cleared a little as they drove down Park Lane past Hyde Park, then stalled as they reached the Wellington Arch. Diana pointed out the rear wall of Buckingham Palace but the group just gazed at it, seemingly unenthusiastic today.

On the south side of the river, they passed the MI6 building overlooking the Thames, prompting a few mutterings about James Bond from Reuben. They carried on through Elephant and Castle, Bermondsey and Deptford, during which Diana gave them an overview of the morning's activity.

"So today's activity will be mudlarking. The foreshore of the River Thames is one of the world's richest archaeological sites and you'll get a chance to explore it for yourselves. We'll be with a local historian who can help you find and identify items of interest."

Gareth looked up. "Which part of the river will we be visiting?"

"We're going to Greenwich. We haven't been over that way yet, and there are plenty of great places to explore afterwards if anyone wants to."

He nodded in approval. "Greenwich is always

pleasant. But had you thought of somewhere more iconic like Tower Bridge?"

"Access to mudlarking is controlled by the Port of London," she told him. "The area by Tower Bridge is out of bounds, even to fully licensed mudlarks."

Reuben had been gazing out of the window, no doubt searching for Romans. He turned to Diana. "It's safe, then?"

"There are hazards," she replied, "but our guide Carolyn will brief us on how to avoid them when we get there."

Zaf walked up and down the bus, giving out gloves to those who didn't have them while Diana finished answering questions.

"We'll need to keep an eye on numbers so we don't lose anyone," she said. "Can you do a regular headcount?"

"I'll set a timer on my phone."

"Good idea." She raised an eyebrow, hoping the tensions of the previous evening were fading. "We don't want any more members of this group dying on our watch."

Newton pulled up in Greenwich and Diana picked up the microphone again. "We'll be leaving the bus here." She pointed towards a grand building. "The river is just the other side of the Royal Naval College. We'll walk around and meet Carolyn by the stairs to the foreshore."

She led the way towards the river. The group dawdled, captivated first by the grand buildings and then by the unexpected sight of old-fashioned rigging.

"What's that?" asked Serena. "Is it an old ship?"

"The Cutty Sark," said Diana. "It's a nineteenth century tea clipper. One of Greenwich's most popular attractions."

"Tea clipper, huh?" said Reuben.

"Built to deliver tea from China as fast as possible," Diana explained. "I gather some of your American ancestors enjoyed tossing crates of the stuff into the sea."

This drew a chuckle.

Diana led them past the pier and along between the river and the college to a set of stone steps beyond the iron railings. A slim, dark-haired woman was waiting for them.

"Carolyn!" Diana waved her duck brolly in greeting. "Good to see you. This is my colleague Zaf, and you'll meet the rest of the group soon enough."

Carolyn put a hand on Diana's arm. "Good to see you too, Diana. I have a treat in store." She turned to the group. "Morning everybody! My name's Carolyn Desanti, and I'm a historian and a Finds Liaison Officer. The tide is out today so we have plenty of foreshore to explore. There shouldn't be anywhere you can get cut off here, but please can you all stay within sight of me, yes?"

The group nodded and mumbled agreement.

"We'll take a slow walk down these steps," said Carolyn.

Diana waited until the last of the group had made it down the steps, slick with pungent green algae. The foreshore was like a beach, sandy in places but with pebbles and stones underfoot in others. A briny seaside smell filled the air.

Carolyn bent to pick up a short white object. "Take a look at this, everyone. It's a fragment of a clay pipe: keep your eyes open and you might find a whole one. Don't forget your gloves."

Everyone stared at the ground. Gareth gave a whoop of delight. "I got one!"

Carolyn applauded. "You might also find animal bones. We can expect sheep, cow, pig, horse. Maybe even boar."

Serena wore an expression of disgust. She took a step back, towards the steps.

"And this passes for entertainment, does it?"

"Another one!" Gareth picked up a second pipe stem.

"Apparently, it does," said Diana, aware that she had a twinkle in her eye.

Chapter Forty

Carolyn gave out more information on what they might find, then gestured around the foreshore.

"Everybody spend a few minutes looking around for yourselves. Come and show me if you find something interesting."

Diana and Zaf headed in opposite directions, like sheepdogs tasked with keeping outliers from straying too far from the main group. Diana found a clay pipe fragment and tried to imagine the Londoner who might have left it there, hundreds of years ago. She knew that clay pipes had been cheap, which accounted for the huge number of them abandoned by the river.

Brie was near her, searching the ground. "It's like being by the sea, isn't it?"

"It is," said Diana.

"Oh Brie, darling, would you give me a hand with this?" Serena called.

Diana hadn't heard Serena say *darling* before. Had her chat with the woman last night done some good?

Brie trotted over. "What is it?"

"Can you pick that up and turn it over, please? I don't want to touch it, it's gross."

Diana drifted over to see what Serena had found.

Brie reached down and flipped the object over with a gloved hand. "I think it's a jawbone."

"Carolyn will know better than me," said Diana, "but I think it's the jawbone of a sheep."

"Just take a picture for me please, Brie," said Serena, her attention already elsewhere.

Diana looked down and tried to relax her gaze. She waited for her brain to alert her to unnatural shapes, circles and straight lines that didn't belong in nature.

Gareth hollered. "A car!"

He held up a tiny car with no wheels but with distinctive seventies styling. He made vrooming sounds as he raced in circles, showing it off.

Diana smiled. Serena shook her head.

"I found a coin!" shouted Reuben, holding it aloft. "Please tell me it's Roman! It's gotta be Roman!"

Diana went over to see the coin he was holding out in his palm.

"Can you wipe off that mud with your thumb?" she asked.

He frowned at her. "Surely this is where we bring in a brush or something? My thumb will be too harsh."

"You can be gentle," she said. "Or maybe give it a little rinse at the edge of the river."

Reuben glanced sideways at the river, then gave his coin the softest swipe with his thumb. He gazed tenderly down at his treasure. "It says something. Let me see. Oh."

"What's it say?" Diana asked.

"Wrangler." Reuben's face fell.

Diana suppressed a smile. "It's a jeans button. Better luck next time. Keep searching."

He dropped the button and went back to scanning the ground, his feet sinking into the silty mud.

"Can I ask you a question?" said Diana as the two of them searched side by side.

"You may."

"Yesterday morning, where were you?"

He straightened up. "Excuse me?"

"The hotel staff are trying to find someone who may have lost something. I wondered if you could tell me where you were."

The accountant pulled back, his expression wary.

"I had breakfast. I spoke with Mr Booncastle and then I was at the theatre later with Serena."

"I'm thinking of around ten fifteen, ten twenty."

Diana wasn't expecting for a moment that Reuben would confess to ransacking Brie Grebbson's room, but she watched his face carefully anyway.

"Um, ten fifteen?" he said, looking away towards the north bank of the river and Canary Wharf beyond.

"Ten fifteen, ten twenty," she repeated.

"I was probably with Ms McNash."

Serena was nearby. She stepped closer to them.

"I went over to the theatre. You said you had to hang back," she said. "Wouldn't it just be easier to tell us what was lost, Diana?"

Diana eyed her: *listening in*.

"Oh, then I was probably chatting with Gareth," said Reuben. "Right, Gareth?"

Across the way, sunk a considerable distance in his tweedy plus-fours but unable to hide his enjoyment at the morning's activity, Gareth looked up.

Diana could have sworn he was opening his mouth to agree when Brie piped up.

"You had that emergency appointment yesterday morning," said the PA. "It's in my calendar. You were unable to attend the morning briefing at the theatre because of that."

"Ah, yes," said Gareth. "Appointment. I did."

Serena looked at him. "Everything's alright, I hope?"

"Yes, yes. Everything's fine. Just an appointment."

"Medical?"

"Medicinal?" suggested Diana, thinking of what she had found in his dressing room.

Gareth shot her a look. "No. An old friend. I had

to see an old friend. Meet a man about a dog and all that."

Diana turned back to Reuben. "So, you weren't with Gareth, Mr Romano. Any thoughts on where you might have been?"

She was surprised to see fear on the accountant's face. She watched him, puzzled.

"I was definitely somewhere," he stammered. "Meeting someone on business."

Diana cocked her head. "You just don't recall who?"

Reuben swallowed hard, his Adam's apple bobbing in his long neck. Diana shared a look with Brie, who was standing very still.

The young woman knew what this meant: Reuben was unaccounted for during the time of the break-in.

Diana was about to press the matter further when a chirpy *bing bong* alarm chimed.

"Time to do a headcount," said Zaf, waving his phone. He totted up the people present. "All here!"

"Well, that's a relief," Serena said. "At least today we know where everyone is."

She gave Reuben a look. Diana watched the two of them, intrigued.

Serena knew something. She absolutely knew something.

Chapter Forty-One

Zaf reset the timer on his phone. Everyone was here, so he could look back at the ground.

Diana had been right about this mudlarking thing being addictive. He picked his way across the foreshore, his face screwed up in concentration.

He spotted something: a piece of terracotta. He bent down to pick it up.

Carolyn peered at it when he approached her.

"Part of a roof tile," she said. "Keep your eyes open for more, that'll help when it comes to dating it. It could be Roman, medieval or later."

"Roman?" said Reuben.

Zaf rolled his eyes and carried on looking. How could roof tiles from so far apart in time look the same?

He heard a noise and looked up to see Gareth

swoop past with his toy car. He was waving it in the air, making vrooming noises like he was five years old.

Actors.

Gareth sped away, making Zaf worry. He'd make sure he looked out for the actor before the next head-count. The idiot would probably have drowned by then.

Suddenly, Gareth stumbled. His foot had hit a stump of wood sticking up from the stones.

Zaf watched as he went down sideways. He ran to catch up with the actor, feeling guilty for what he'd been thinking.

As Zaf ran, Gareth bellowed like he was dying on stage.

Was he seriously injured? Or just doing his actor thing?

Zaf caught up and grabbed Gareth's arm. Gareth dragged him down into the mud.

Eww. Zaf was wearing one of the shirts he'd picked up from Diana's neighbour's flat. It was ruined.

But a guest was injured.

"Are you OK?" he breathed.

Gareth said nothing. His face was pale.

Carolyn appeared next to them. "I'm a first aider. Let me check him over."

Zaf pushed himself up, trying not to think about the state of his clothes. Diana and the others had joined them and were clustered around.

Zaf kneeled beside Carolyn on the stones, ready to help. She pushed a fleece under Gareth's head.

"Tell me your name, sweetheart," she said.

"Oh please," replied Gareth, wincing. "I think we all know who I am. Gareth Booncastle. My mind is perfectly alright, but I'm afraid my leg might not be."

"Right, well, I'll check you over and call for an ambulance if you're injured."

"I cannot permit that! I'm performing tonight. The show must go on."

Zaf was still next to Gareth and Carolyn. Did actors really say that?

"By all means perform your checks," Gareth declared, "but I absolutely cannot be carried away on a stretcher. The gutter press would have a field day."

Carolyn's jaw clenched, but she continued to examine Gareth's leg, talking softly to him the whole time. Every time she touched his leg, he howled.

Diana was at the front of the group. She bent to murmur in Carolyn's ear. "Shall I make that call?"

"No ambulance!" Gareth said. "Many an actor has been ruined by being photographed in an incapacitated state. If you help me up the stairs and into a taxi then I can avoid the paps."

Zaf looked up and around them. "There's no paps here." He stood up and shook off the worst of the mud. "It's just us."

"No paps! That's what they want you to think.

The sniff of an ambulance and they'll be straight here, I know them."

"But the stairs, mate, it's not safe—"

"A couple of strong people will have me up those stairs in a jiffy."

Carolyn sat back on her heels, her examination complete. "I can't see much else wrong with you apart from your leg, Gareth, but you should get yourself checked out at a hospital. I strongly advise you to let us call the paramedics."

"Carolyn." Gareth extended a hand to clasp hers. "Many thanks for your tender ministrations, but I cannot permit that to happen. Now, who will be my shoulder-bearers?"

"I'll do it," said Zaf. He looked around to see who else might be strong enough. No one stepped forward.

Carolyn sighed. "I'll help. My first aid training might be useful. Come on."

They made their way up the slippery stairs, Gareth wincing at the movement. There were benches along the walkway at the top. They helped Gareth onto one.

"How are you doing?" asked Carolyn. "Feeling light-headed at all?"

"No. Apart from this wretched leg, I feel fine."

"I've called a taxi," said Diana just as one pulled up behind them.

"Oi, oi, Miss Bakewell," called the cabby from the window. "Where's this one going?"

Zaf looked round. Since when did cabs just turn up like that?

But this wasn't just any cab.

The driver was Chaz Chase, Ernie's gofer and occasional barman. Zaf gave Diana a look. *You're a miracle worker.* That was one way of looking at it, at least.

"Queen Elizabeth Hospital in Woolwich," said Diana.

Zaf and Carolyn helped Gareth into the taxi, while Chaz looked on, his eyes narrowed.

"Zaf, can you go with him?" said Diana. "One of us needs to stay with the group."

He nodded.

"No fuss," hissed Gareth through gritted teeth. "No fuss."

"It's fine." Zaf clambered in with him.

Chaz turned to look at them in the back seat. "You getting mud on my polished leather?"

Zaf looked down at himself. "I'm pretty much all mud now."

"We'll come to an arrangement, Chaz," Diana said through the front window.

"Right you are," said the driver and pulled away from the kerb.

"I'm not going to hospital," said Gareth.

Chaz looked at them in his rear-view mirror. "Miss Bakewell said."

"I'll give you fifty to just take me home. Camden Town."

"Camden Town from here'll cost you a hundred, mate." Chaz's eyes narrowed again, his gaze still on Gareth. "Oh, it's you, squire. Didn't recognise you with all the mud."

Zaf saw Gareth's expression shift. The man clearly enjoyed being recognised, but hadn't been expecting it here.

"Duchess of Limehouse," said the shaven-headed driver. "Behind the bar. Chaz."

"Oh. Yes. Yes, of course," replied Gareth.

"How did the meeting go with Mr Spielberg yesterday?"

Gareth's jaw clenched. He glanced at Zaf. "It wasn't Steven himself. It was an associate, a go-between. Just a chat between professionals."

Zaf shrugged. "Met a man about a dog, huh?"

"An Oscar-worthy dog if you must know."

Gareth shifted his body, wincing as he did so. He turned his back on Zaf and gazed out of the window.

Fine with me. Zaf wasn't in the mood for polite conversation. He watched the streets go by as they headed north for Camden.

A few minutes and just twelve miles later, the taxi pulled up on Regents Park Road. Zaf peered out, admiring the tall Georgian houses.

Gareth passed Chaz a handful of notes. He pushed open the taxi door.

"D'you want a hand?" Zaf asked.

Gareth shook his head. He dragged himself onto the pavement, hissing and quietly cursing.

When he was at last upright and the door was closed, he bent to look through the open window. "Tell them I will be on stage tonight, no matter what!"

Zaf nodded.

"You 'opping out here an' all?" said Chaz.

"I need to go home and clean up. Eccleston Square."

Chaz nodded. "And do you have a hundred quid fare on you?"

"No."

"And have you twisted your knee, mate?"

"Er, no."

Chaz sucked through his teeth. "Then may I suggest that it's a fine day for a walk through Regents Park. Won't take you more than an hour."

Zaf pulled in a heavy breath.

"I'm saying hop it, mate." Chaz had turned in his seat and was giving Zaf a friendly grin: *nothing personal.*

"Fine." Zaf got out.

Chaz pulled away, doing one of those tight U-turns that only London cabs could manage.

Zaf looked up at the sky and peeled a heavy fleck of foreshore mud off his lapel. Chaz was right about one thing. It would be a fine day for a walk.

Chapter Forty-Two

The mudlarking had been disrupted by Gareth's accident, but it didn't take long after his departure for the group to return to searching the foreshore in silence Diana watched them, wondering if the quiet was due to worry about their colleague or simply concentration.

Serena approached her. "I do hope Gareth's better very soon. I'm certain it will be no more than a sprain."

Diana nodded. "A bit of rest will see him right, I'm sure."

Serena frowned. "The man is on stage later. I don't believe the British production can withstand any further upsets."

"No. And he was so keen to join us with the mudlarking."

"I have to hand it to you Diana, this activity has been so much better than I'd imagined."

"Why, thank you." Diana was unused to such kindness from the woman. "I hope we've managed to entertain you."

"Very much so."

"And I know this week hasn't really gone to plan. The Londiniumarium was a disappointment, and I hope no one from Chartwell and Crouch tours has... has rubbed you up the wrong way." She thought of Zaf's challenge in the theatre, and his loyalty to Brie.

"Pfft. Think nothing of it." Serena straightened and looked across the shining wet foreshore at her accountant. "Some things have gone entirely as planned."

"Oh?" said Diana.

"I could have brought any one of a number of money men with me. But I took a gamble on my ex-brother-in-law..."

Ex-brother in-law. Diana was about to open her mouth when there was a yelp of excitement from Reuben.

"A coin! A coin!"

Brie, who'd been searching close to him, hurried to his side. Carolyn came over to inspect it.

"I think... Wipe it slowly, yes that's it." The historian smiled. "Well done, you've found a Roman coin. Looks like copper. Could be a sestertius."

Diana and Serena shared a glance. They were never going to hear the end of this.

"A real ancient find, as held by my ancestors!" Reuben cried, waving the coin aloft.

"Um, possibly," said Carolyn. "Let's see." She brushed away more dirt. "I can't quite make out the legend, but I'd say that's possibly an image of Antoninus Pius."

"Antoninus Pius," breathed Reuben, his face alight.

"Father of Marcus Aurelias," Diana said to Serena. "One of the so-called 'good emperors'."

"So, it's a real ancient coin," Serena replied. "An antique."

Diana shrugged. "You could probably pick one up for less than fifty quid from a dealer. Those Romans had lots of holes in their pockets."

Serena laughed, then composed herself.

"It's made him happy," she said. "Fascinating to know we're walking around on all this history."

"Most of London's like that," Diana said. "Every corner of this city has a story to tell."

Serena gave her a shrewd look. "Knowing what that story is. That's the key that unlocks everything, isn't it?"

Diana frowned. Once again, she had the feeling Serena was hinting at something she wasn't prepared to share.

Serena leaned in. "You will come to the show tonight. I hope."

"Me?" Diana replied. "That's very kind."

"You and your young colleague. A thank you from us."

"Tha—"

"A roman coin! See! I knew it!"

She looked up to see Reuben dancing around the foreshore, approaching each member of the group in turn and showing them the coin.

At least the afternoon's activity had made some people happy.

Chapter Forty-Three

The walk home took Zaf over Primrose Hill, where he paused to take in the view of central London, and then through Regent's Park. By the time he was walking down Baker Street towards Oxford Street, the sun had dried his wet knees and the clods of mud had mostly fallen off.

He decided he was presentable enough for a bus and got onto a number 2 that took him most of the way home to Pimlico. By the time he reached the tall house in Eccleston Square he was tired but in a much better mood than he had been when Chaz had refused him a lift.

As he opened the front door, he found the landlord, Alexsei, standing in the communal hallway. Zaf was beginning to suspect Alexsei lurked there on purpose, just to make some sort of point.

"Hello, Alexsei."

Alexsei cocked his head. "Home in the day? You were sacked perhaps?"

Zaf frowned, hoping Alexsei was joking. "No, there was a... an incident. I got mud on my trousers. I came back to get changed."

"I heard you and Diana arguing."

"I don't know if I'd call it arguing."

"Raised voices. There are thick walls and floors here. *Good bones,* as the estate agents say. But I heard."

Zaf sighed. The landlord was looking at his face with those dark eyes, and it felt disconcertingly like he was trying to read Zaf's mind.

"Yes," he admitted. "We argued yesterday."

But the argument had been interrupted. And things had been fine since then.

Hadn't they?

Yes. They had. Zaf liked Diana and he believed she liked him. They made good colleagues. Maybe not such good flatmates, though.

"We argued," he continued. "But it cleared the air. Sometimes people have things they need to work out between them. I mean, it's healthy, right?" Zaf cursed inwardly. *Don't sound so needy.*

"Diana is too good," Alexsei said. "Too kind. I have told her as much."

Zaf looked the landlord in the eye. "I'm not taking advantage of her. I've told her I'm moving out."

"Oh. When?"

"We... We started to discuss it and then things came up. We haven't fixed a date."

"You have not fixed a date." Alexsei shook his head. "And this is how it goes on. She is too good, too willing to see the good side."

Zaf could feel his muscles tensing. How was this Alexsei's business?

A thought hit him: could Alexsei kick him out? Tell Diana she wasn't allowed to sublet?

But he wasn't paying her. He was a guest. Not a tenant.

That makes it worse.

"I *am* good," he said. "I am nice."

"Excellent," Alexsei replied with a smile. "Then make your plans to leave and stick to it. I will not stand to see her hurt again."

"Hurt?"

Alexsei frowned. His dark eyebrows came together, almost kissing.

"You know, the whole Morris Walker thing."

Zaf did not know *the whole Morris Walker thing.* But he knew who Morris Walker was.

"I've heard that name before," he said. "He was the boss at the tour company."

"Boss, yeah? Look where he is now."

"Where *is* he now?"

Alexsei gave him a *how stupid are you?* look. "His Majesty's Prison, Pentonville."

Zaf narrowed his eyes. He'd overhead Diana and

Ernie talking about this, when they'd been investigating a death in the Houses of Parliament.

"What happened?" he asked.

Alexsei shook his head. "The point is, she put her faith in him. She staked her reputation on him. Even when all the signs were there, even when he was clearly taking advantage of her good nature, she stood by him."

"I see," said Zaf, not quite seeing at all.

"If you want to hurt her, she will let you hurt her."

Zaf nodded. He felt like he'd just been told off by the headteacher. Or by his mum.

"You... you clearly care for her," he said. "That's not normally the role of a landlord."

Alexsei shrugged. A tiny smile played at his lips. Zaf noticed for the first time that he could be quite handsome, in the right light.

And in the right mood.

"She is a good person," Alexsei said. "Too good, yes, but she is a good person. I did not grow up surrounded by good people. I do not know many good people." He gestured through the open door at the garden that dominated the centre of Eccleston Square. "She tends to the flowers. She goes to the gardens and flowerboxes of empty houses with absent owners. She prunes and cultivates and encourages and protects."

"I know. It's a bit of a thankless task."

Alexsei nodded. "Too good. And so, I see her and I encourage her as much as I can and I protect her as much as I am able." He looked Zaf up and down. "I think you might be a good person."

"I am. I swear."

A shrug. "And if you are that good person, maybe you can be encouraged, too. Or, if not, you can be pruned."

Zaf gave the landlord a smile. "I get you. Anyway, I need to get changed."

He backed away and made his way up the stairs.

His phone buzzed as he reached the first landing. He fished it out of his jacket pocket: a message from Diana.

Get your glad rags on. We're going to the theatre tonight.

Zaf smiled, considering what he'd wear. His best trousers were caked in mud and he'd messed up two jackets, one with mud and the other with expensive pickle.

He glanced up the stairs to the top floor flat. Most of Bryan's belongings had been sorted and cleared out now, but there several trunks of clothes waiting to go to vintage stores or charity shops.

Zaf ran over their contents in his mind. The clothes were psychedelic, joyful. Just what he needed.

He set about getting washed and changed.

Chapter Forty-Four

Diana stopped the group at the entrance to the Redhouse Hotel. Newton had already started the bus up again, and was pulling out into the traffic.

"Please everyone, try to remove what mud you can before we go inside."

The group stopped to wipe their feet, stomp on the doormat, or bash their shoes against the wall. She surveyed their efforts, knowing Penny would appreciate not having her foyer covered in mud.

She watched the bus recede into the traffic, imagining Newton's face right now. The instant he arrived at the depot, he would be getting out his broom and his special cloths. He'd visibly twitched when he'd seen the state of the group after the mudlarking.

"Two and a half hours before we gather in reception,"

she announced as the group passed her. They looked tired and hungry, but there was a big night ahead. Some of them had meetings, and then there was the evening performance of *The Cockney's Complaint* to look forward to.

Diana had heard most of it in rehearsals and was looking forward to seeing the whole thing played out from start to finish.

After a brief word with Penny, she walked to the Chartwell and Crouch depot. She had two hours to change for the evening performance. In theory she could go home in that time, but she knew there was a change of clothes hanging in her work locker. *Always be prepared*, that was her motto.

She washed in the little sink in the women's toilets and shrugged on a burnt orange velvet jacket over a plain silk top. The trousers she'd worn during the day worked well once she'd used a clothes brush to spruce them up. She checked herself in the mirror, reapplied some makeup and stood back.

You'll do.

She checked her watch: three quarters of an hour to spare. She was hungry.

She left the depot, waving to Newton who was polishing the floor of the bus, and walked to the *Tasty For You* café at the end of the street. She was partway through ordering a sandwich from Levon behind the counter when she noticed Paul Kensington sitting alone at a table by the window.

She hesitated. He hadn't seen her. And this was Paul Kensington, a man who was not known for his social skills.

But she was Diana Bakewell. A woman who *was* well known for her social skills.

She approached the table. "Paul."

He looked up. His expression was blank for a moment, but then he recognised her and a twitch of irritation crossed his face. "Diana."

She gave him the best smile she could muster.

"Good afternoon," he said, his tone stiff. He didn't gesture for her to join him.

"Hello." Diana glanced across at the counter where Levon was making her sandwich, oblivious.

At last, Paul gestured at the chair opposite. "Would you like to sit?"

"I wouldn't want to intrude."

What she meant was *no*. But Diana was too polite for *no*.

"It's fine," he said. "Actually, I have a question for you."

Diana had been preparing an excuse. But now he'd piqued her interest.

She thought back to DCI Sugarbrook calling her *nosey* and frowned. Diana wasn't *nosey*. She had a healthy interest in people.

And this, whatever it was, might affect her job.

She sat down opposite Paul, just as Levon appeared with her sandwich. He placed it on the table between her and her boss, along with a cup of tea.

Paul leaned back, his eyes narrowing as she picked up her sandwich. "Did the mudskipping go well today?"

"Mudlarking," Diana replied, disappointed. "Was that the question?"

"No."

"It went very well." She decided not to mention Gareth Booncastle falling over and dramatically hurting his knee.

"That's good. That's good," he said, pulling his chair forward and casting his gaze downward.

Diana wasn't in the habit of socialising with Paul Kensington. He reminded her of a corporate Power-Point presentation: all bullet points and buzzwords but lacking any detail or substance. He hid away in his office until he had to emerge from his shell and bark out little orders, but otherwise, he didn't engage with colleagues and employees. Not really.

"I want to ask you about the Londiniumarium," he said.

"An awful name," she said. "An awful name for an awful thing."

"It should be an amazing success."

"Should it?"

"I'm honestly baffled as to why it's *not* a success."

"You *are?*"

Irritation crossed his face, swiftly overtaken by the

tired confusion that seemed to have become his default expression.

"People love London," he said.

"They do," Diana agreed, taking a bite of her sandwich. She hadn't realised how hungry she was, and she wasn't about to let Paul Kensington get in the way of addressing that.

"The idea behind the Londiniumarium is to take all the very best bits of London and make copies of them and put them all in one place. How can that not be a good thing?"

Diana stared at her boss for a long, long moment.

"Oh, Paul. Do you... do you actually think that's how things work?"

"Well... Yes."

She shook her head. "London is Big Ben and St Paul's and the Thames and Oxford Street and Hyde Park and the London Eye and Tower Bridge and the Millennium Dome and so much more. And those, to differing degrees, are all wonderful things." She set her sandwich down on the plate, feeling her heart swell at the thought of her beloved city. "But Big Ben isn't the world's tallest or grandest clock tower. St Paul's is not the world's largest dome. The Thames is neither the widest nor longest nor prettiest river."

He wrinkled his nose. "I didn't expect you to say that."

"London is no one thing," Diana said. "London is a pulsing, living thing, with millions of working parts that do just that... work." She sighed. "And making a copy of individual parts of it is missing the point entirely."

"Any creative endeavour involves some copying."

"True." What was it Serena had said? *All art is plagiarism, my dear.* "But it's how you put those pieces together. People know when they're being sold a fake. They feel it in their guts."

Paul Kensington shook his head, his hands twiddling in his lap. Diana couldn't tell if he was questioning his own commitment to the Londiniumarium or questioning her opinion on it.

"Art," she said, "any creativity. It's fickle. That's how you can have a hit musical like *The Cockney's Complaint* on one side of the street and that Dick Whittington musical everyone hates on the other. There's no magic formula for success." She leaned forward. Did he really not understand? "And if there was one, then the Londiniumarium has missed it by a mile."

Paul sighed. "And here was me hoping it would be the saving of us."

Diana felt her muscles tense. "Do we need saving?"

He tightened his jaw. "The happy carefree days of Morris Walker's stewardship are behind us now. Chartwell and Crouch must adapt or die."

Diana swallowed the rest of her cup of tea in one

go and placed the remainder of her sandwich back in its bag.

"If that's the case," she said, "perhaps it's better to die with dignity than to survive as something monstrous."

She left the café and walked to the Redhouse Hotel, nibbling at her sandwich as she walked. It would have been so much nicer eating it at *Tasty For You*. But she didn't want to discuss the Londiniumarium for a single second longer.

At the hotel, Zaf was waiting by the reception desk. He was dressed in a sharp retro suit with a colourful shirt.

She smiled. "A dash of wartime spiv and a smidgeon of swinging sixties Carnaby Street."

He looked down at himself. "I was going for rakish jazz saxophonist."

"Yes, that too." She brushed a fleck of dirt off his lapel. "It looks good on you. Bryan would have liked to see another man enjoying his clothes."

"As long as you don't mind," he said.

She smiled. "Bryan's old clothes are one thing in my home you are absolutely welcome to help yourself to. Did you get Gareth to hospital?"

"He insisted on going home. He was limping, but he could move, so I'd imagine he hasn't broken anything."

Diana remembered something. "He was limping this morning."

"Gareth? When?"

"On his way here." She looked at Zaf, her mind racing. "And then he saw me and he stopped."

Zaf chewed his bottom lip. "So he was already injured. He did seem to be howling more than you'd expect when he fell on the shoreline. But, if he'd already hurt himself..."

Diana was considering what that might mean when they were interrupted by Serena's arrival. The producer had changed into a violet dress with embroidered detail on the bodice and a skirt that swirled as she walked.

Brie, still wearing her trousers and blouse from earlier, trotted up behind her, carrying a violet handbag. "I found the bag, Serena."

"About time." Serena took the bag and transferred items from the brown bag she'd been carrying into the violet one. "Please put this one away."

Diana watched the younger woman as she retreated towards the stairs. Would she have time to change before the performance, or would she be too busy servicing Serena's needs?

Diana and Zaf waited for the rest of the party to assemble. Reuben had a folded handkerchief in his hand. He stood next to Diana, opened it and held it out. The crusty ancient Roman coin was inside.

"A prize worth treasuring," she said.

"Absolutely." He folded the handkerchief up and tucked it in the breast pocket of his jacket.

Diana grabbed an envelope from Penny's counter. "Perhaps it might be safer to put the coin in here."

"Really?"

"Better that than it fall out of your hankie and get lost on the floor or sucked up by a hoover."

"Hoover?"

"A vacuum cleaner."

Reuben shrugged and took the envelope from her.

She heard the bus pulling up outside and led the group out to the pavement. Newton had given the old Routemaster one of the most thorough clean-downs she'd ever seen. He'd also placed a cat carrier on a seat at the front.

She gave him a questioning look.

"Operation Eagle's Nest," he said.

"Pardon?"

"I'm going to go in and rescue Gus from the theatre."

"Er, OK. And Eagle's Nest?"

"Every successful operation needs a suitable name."

Chapter Forty-Five

The bus drove them past the vast screens of Piccadilly Circus, the theatre hoardings of the West End and the decorations of the adjacent Chinatown. It wasn't hard to be infected by the glitz and excitement of it all, Zaf thought.

As they stepped off the bus, one of the Delphinium's door staff gave a little salute and opened an additional door for the group.

"Is Mr Booncastle fit and well for tonight's performance?" Serena asked the woman.

The woman gave a shrug. "As far as I'm aware. Understudy's not been called."

"Very good."

Zaf slipped in at the back of the group, enjoying the feeling of being a guest and not a tour guide. Diana was at the front, looking around, taking everything in.

They went straight to the small public bar where an even smaller area had been roped off for VIP pre-performance drinks. Serena's drink was already waiting for her on the bar.

The perks of wealth and status, thought Zaf.

As Serena picked up her drink, Charlotte the theatre manager and Noah the composer approached the group.

"Good evening," said Charlotte. "It's a delight to have you all here."

The group shook hands with the pair and exchanged greetings. Zaf thought of the last time they'd socialised in a group like this, and how that had been interrupted by Todd Granger plummeting to his death.

He gave a little shudder. There would be nothing like that tonight. Tonight was about kicking back and enjoying himself.

He shuffled towards the bar alongside Diana and ordered a tonic water for her and a San Miguel for himself.

"So are we off-duty now?" he asked her.

She turned to him. "We're still representing Chartwell and Crouch. And, by extension, the Delphinium. Don't forget, they're footing the bill for all this."

"OK. Best behaviour."

Diana raised an eyebrow. "You're not on your best behaviour all the time?"

Zaf let out a breath. Sometimes, it was impossible

to relax around Diana. "It's a sliding scale. Being good takes effort." He hesitated. "You know, you're not perfect either."

"Of course I'm not."

Zaf lowered his voice. "Something Alexsei said earlier..."

"Yes?" Diana wasn't making eye contact, but her face was tense.

"He's very protective of you."

"Is he?" She smiled. "He's a sweet boy."

Not so much of the boy. "Worships the ground you walk on, more like."

She glanced at him. "Has he taken my side against you?"

Zaf shrugged. "It's OK. I'm moving out, aren't I?"

"Is that really necessary?"

"It's that," he said, "or we argue till one of us goes mad."

Diana laughed. "I'm not sure it's gone quite that far, Zaf." She turned to him. "We have to resolve this thing between us. You're not ready to move out yet."

"You're my mum now?"

"OK." She shook her head. "Let me rephrase that. You don't have *enough money* to move out yet. You need to find somewhere to rent. And in the meantime, we need to sort things out between us."

"But we're too spikey to discuss things properly."

"Too true." Diana was surveying the group: smiles

here and nods there. Ever the attentive tour guide. But Zaf knew he had her attention.

He put his beer down on the counter. "We should have a FessHole."

"A *what*?"

"A FessHole. Like a confessional."

"FessHole." Her nose wrinkled. "You've just made that word up."

"Nope. We write things down that we feel bad about and we put them in a place where everyone can see them. It's anonymous so we don't really know who wrote what, but it means we can get stuff out of our system."

Diana stared hard at him. "How would that whole 'anonymous' thing work when there are only two of us in the flat?"

"Fair point."

"But," Diana said, "a place where we can vent our frustrations could be helpful."

She dug into her handbag and brought out a Redhouse Hotel envelope. "Here. I gave one of these to Reuben Romano for his coin, but this one's going spare."

Zaf looked at the envelope. "We write things down and put them in that?"

"Yes. So we'd only read them when we're feeling... robust, and adult. It will give us a window into what's causing a problem without having an actual argument." She licked her lips. "Let's start now."

Diana waved the barman over and asked for some paper. He smiled at her – *yet another of her acquaintances*, Zaf thought – and handed one over. She thanked him and tore it into ticket-sized stubs.

Zaf watched as Diana bent over one of the sheets of paper, writing on it with a pen she'd taken from her bag. A Londiniumarium pen, he noticed.

At last she finished. She straightened up, folded it into four and wrote Zaf on it. She placed the folded-up scrap of paper into the envelope.

Zaf was about to speak when Diana took another of the sheets of paper. He waited while she wrote out two more sheets, folded them all up and put them in the envelope.

When she was done, he cleared his throat. "So each one of those is something about me that annoys you?"

"It is."

We'll see about that, then.

Zaf pulled a pile of papers towards himself and began to write. While he did so, Diana filled out more. After a few minutes he'd written four sheets, while she had six.

He tapped the envelope, unsure if he regretted having suggested this. "All our deep dark secrets in here."

Brie and Noah Dart were rwatching them. "What are you two doing?" Noah asked.

Zaf turned to him. "Writing down what we hate about each other."

"You're wh—"

"Not hate, exactly," Diana interrupted. "We're just writing down the things that irritate us."

"Is this some wacky British pastime I've somehow forgotten?" Brie asked.

"No British pastime I know of," said Noah.

"No," said Diana. "No, it's..."

She stopped talking, her hand on the envelope. Zaf waited. Noah and Brie's eyes were on her, waiting too.

She looked down at the envelope. "Hoover."

"Come again?" said Brie.

She took in a sharp breath and looked at Brie, her expression intense. "A coin would get sucked up by a hoover."

"Sorry?" said Noah.

"Something small, something flat. Like a coin. It might get sucked up."

Zaf frowned. Brie had a confused look on her face.

"Sorry," he said. "She normally makes more sense than this."

Diana turned the envelope over in her hands. She stared at it. "The housekeeping woman at the hotel. She went into your room twice, Brie."

"Yes," Brie said. "And?"

"She went to empty the hoover bag. It was making a noise. Like something had got sucked up inside it that shouldn't have been there. And the thing that's missing from your room, the gift from Todd Granger, the thing the burglar was looking for. It was small enough to fit in an envelope, small enough to fall down the back of a dressing table, small enough to get sucked up by a hoover."

"They were looking for a coin?" Zaf said.

"No." Diana shook her head. "Maybe. Or something else. The point is, what if the item that's missing was in the hoover bag?"

"And then in the bin, and now thrown out," he said.

"I'm not so sure. The hoover gets emptied into a bin, yes."

"What's all of this about?" said Noah.

Diana ignored him. "A hotel produces a lot of rubbish in a day."

"But where does Carmen empty the hoover?" Zaf asked.

"Carmen?" asked Brie.

"The maid," Diana said.

"Diana has this memory for people," Zaf explained. "Worms her way into their hearts. Honestly, by this time next week, she and Carmen will be the best of friends."

"You need to go," Diana told him.

"Go? Go back to the hotel?" He had a realisation that made his heart sink. "Go bin-diving?"

Diana was looking at Brie. "Do you not want to know what the thing is? The thing that Todd possibly sent you, the thing that fell on the floor and got sucked up by a hoover?"

"I do," said Brie. "I want to know. I'll come with you."

Zaf glanced aside to where Serena was chatting with Charlotte and Reuben. "You're not needed here?"

"What's she gonna do?" Brie asked, her tone casual. "Fire me?"

"Fair enough," he said. "Let's go bin-diving. Modern history's version of mudlarking."

"I'll hail us a cab," said Noah.

Zaf looked at him. "Us?"

Noah grinned. "Funnily enough, I've seen this musical. I don't need to see it again. But this... this sounds like an adventure."

A voice was telling them to take their seats, over the PA.

"OK," Zaf said to Diana.

"I'm sorry. You'll miss the performance."

"I've seen most of it in rehearsals."

She smiled at him, her eyes alight. "That's the spirit. Good luck."

Chapter Forty-Six

Diana and the American visitors had been allocated a box to watch the performance. Drinks were already waiting on a small table at the back.

Diana had often wondered about the merits of theatre boxes. It wasn't as if they gave the best view, right there above one side of the stage. She imagined it was more about being seen than it was about seeing.

"Where are our young friends?" Reuben asked, indicating Zaf and Brie's empty chairs.

"On a last-minute errand with Noah," Diana replied.

"Ah."

"Going to find something that was lost, I hope. Could I see that coin of yours again?"

"Of course." Reuben produced the envelope, and the sestertius inside.

"Impressive." Diana lifted her phone to take a picture, leaning back to make sure Reuben's face was in shot.

She forwarded the image to Zaf with a message. *If you can, ask Carmen if this was the man in the room.*

"That's quite a find," Charlotte said to Reuben. She brushed his arm with her fingertips.

Message sent, Diana put her phone away. Hopefully things would become clearer very soon.

It turned out Diana had been wrong about the box. The seats gave an excellent view of both auditorium and stage. She scanned the seats as they waited for the show to begin, aware that Newton was out there somewhere, searching for his beloved cat.

I just hope he doesn't disrupt the performance.

There was no sign of him. Diana breathed a sigh of relief and sipped her drink.

The house lights went down and a swell of excited appreciation rippled through the audience. The pit orchestra set up with a lively overture, the curtain rose, and a dozen Cockney market folk ambled onto stage in the manner of everyday people who just happened to be prepared to leap into song at any moment.

Among them, with a swagger that drew attention more effectively than any spotlight, came Gareth Booncastle as Jack Ha'penny. His thumbs were tucked into his ragged lapels, a knotted scarf was tied around his neck, and he wore a flat cap on his head. He was doing an impressive job of suppressing the limp he'd had earlier.

Charlotte leaned over to whisper to Diana. "Our Gareth seems none the worse for his accident. If he'd actually broken that leg messing around by the river, I'd have had to kill him. And then you."

"Quite," Diana whispered in reply. "Although he did insist on coming."

Charlotte snorted. "He's never been the easiest to work with. More than once his antics reduced Todd to tears in his office."

Diana frowned. "Todd didn't have an office."

The performers were dancing, skirts swirling and costermonger baskets spinning, building up to the opening number.

"It was a standing joke," Charlotte whispered. "No space for a director's office. So Todd used to go to hide in the storeroom next to the star dressing rooms."

Chapter Forty-Seven

Zaf's journey back to the hotel was swift and straightforward. The crowd on the tube was now a mixture of late commuters and a more eclectic evening crowd. He stood in silence with Brie and Noah, all of them anxious to be back at the hotel.

They hurried from Baker Street station to the Redhouse Hotel. Zaf was relieved to see Penny Slipper still at reception. It seemed she was glued to the counter from dawn till dusk.

He rushed in, panting.

"Hoover... hoover bag..."

"And a warm welcome to the Redhouse Hotel to you," replied Penny with a smile.

"We need to find the bins," breathed Brie.

Penny blinked, her polite smile just about managing to stay on. She looked at Noah, who had been bringing up the rear.

He approached the counter, noticing Penny's gaze on him. "Oh, don't look at me," he said. "I'm just here for japes."

Zaf regained control of his breath. "There was a maid cleaning Brie's room. Is she here?"

"Oh, that. We call them housekeeping staff or service staff, not maids. And, no, Carmen isn't here right now."

"Diana's sent me a photo we could show her. Maybe it's the man."

Penny nodded. "Blast it over to me care of the hotel enquiries e-mail." Her finger tapped a brochure beneath the glass on the counter. "And the hoover thing?"

"You told Diana that Carmen emptied her hoover that morning. We think the lost item might have been sucked up."

Realisation dawned on Penny's face. "Oh..." She gestured over her shoulder. "There's a whole fleet of wheelie bins out back. Your chances of finding anything are..." She bit her bottom lip. "No. If she was on the first floor, she might have..." She nodded, drumming her fingers on the desk. "Follow me."

She rounded the desk and led them along a back corridor, to a stairway that descended into a cellar.

"The hotel building's old," she said. "It opened in 1883. We're proud of the original features, but..."

They were in a starkly lit service area under the hotel now. Zaf looked around, not sure why she'd led them here.

"It's not always the most practical," Penny continued. "Cleaning and service staff are supposed to carry waste up and down with them these days, but there's always a chance Carmen used one of the chutes."

"Chute?" said Zaf. "Like a laundry chute?"

"Kind of. These are dust chutes, from back when fireplaces needed sweeping on a daily basis. They're designed for ash. Not big enough for rubbish."

Three dumpy wheeled bins sat to one side of the corridor, each positioned beneath a rectangular metal chute.

"There's a chute hatch on every floor," said Penny. "They all connect up, then end up here."

Zaf approached the bins. They were full of rubbish, mostly dry. *Thank goodness.*

He took up position in front of the bin on the left, took off his jacket and rolled up his sleeves. "OK."

"No," said Penny. "I can't let members of the public root around in our rubbish."

"I'm not a member of the public."

She stared at him for a moment, then nodded. "Not like that. I'll fetch you some gloves."

Penny hurried away. Noah was standing beside Zaf, grinning. Brie was shifting from foot to foot, eyeing the bins like she might dive into them at any moment.

"This is certainly an unexpected night's entertainment," said Noah.

"Not that different from the mudlarking," said Brie. She glanced towards where Penny had disappeared, then took off her jacket.

Chapter Forty-Eight

Diana found the experience of watching the show from a box fascinating. There was a pleasant intimacy to being part of a smaller group. And plenty of opportunity to observe the others.

One seat along, Charlotte's hand was resting gently in Reuben's.

Yes, thought Diana. *That might explain a lot.*

After the first couple of songs, she became absorbed. Every now and then, her attention would be diverted by sounds from below.

Someone in the audience was whispering. She craned her neck to see but couldn't make out the culprit.

Be quiet, she thought. *Let us enjoy the show.*

People who insisted on providing their own commentary were such a nuisance.

Halfway through the third song, someone directly below stood up from his seat and shouted out. An attendant appeared, and the man sat down.

Diana peered down into the darkness, unable to concentrate on the show. She thought she recognised a man, not the one who'd stood up from his seat.

This man was walking between the rows, beaming a torch at the ground and shuffling along in a crouched position.

She felt a stab of recognition and looked up at the faces of her companions.

Had they recognised him?

"Oh, Newton," she whispered.

"Is everything OK?" asked Charlotte, who'd been looking at the stage.

Diana nodded. "Excuse me a moment." She slipped out of the box.

Outside the box, she looked along the corridor they'd used to get here. She'd become familiar with the theatre's layout, and knew where to go.

She took a flight of stairs down to the circle, where she found two attendants talking at the entrance.

"Can you smell something like tuna?" said the shorter woman.

"Tuna?" repeated her companion, who was tall with thin dark hair. "Why on earth would there be tuna?"

A member of the audience stalked out of the auditorium. The ruddy-faced man looked like he might explode at any moment.

He stared at the tall attendant. "There's a dashed idiot in there, flicking tuna all over the place and making cat noises!"

"That seems unlikely," said Diana.

He turned to her, his eyes wide. "Are you calling me a liar, woman?"

"Now, sir..." said the shorter attendant. She pulled a walkie talkie out of her pocket.

Her colleague put a hand on her shoulder. "I *can* smell tuna, though."

The short attendant – *Mary*, her badge said – put her walkie talkie away and turned towards the door to the Circle just as it opened and Newton Crombie hurried through. A member of staff was pursing him.

"Sir, you can't—"

Newton turned to the man. Diana realised he was carrying Gus.

He's found him. She found herself smiling with relief. The bus depot hadn't been the same without their tuna-eating feline companion.

"He's with me," she told the three attendants in her best teacher voice. She put a hand on Newton's arm.

"I suggest you take him back to the depot, *now*."

Newton nodded. His cheeks were red and his eyes wet. "I found him, Diana. I found him." He bent and gave the cat a rub on the top of the head with his chin. Gus purred in response.

"I know," she said. "I'm glad."

Chapter Forty-Nine

Something had been troubling Diana, preventing her from enjoying the show as she should have done. And now she was out of her seat, it was time to get some answers about that something.

Watching rehearsals meant she'd got to know the theatre well, and even in the middle of a live performance, she found her way backstage in a matter of minutes. The cast's rendition of *The Old Dog and Duck* accompanied her, muffled by the walls of the corridors.

Back here, crew were mostly invisible, in position or moving silently. Diana looked up towards the lighting rigs at the back of the stage. Up there was the door Todd had stepped through, the gantry he had tumbled over.

It was a chilling thought.

Along the backmost corridor were the dressing rooms, and between them the storeroom she'd discovered the other day. She went inside and flicked on the light.

If this had been Todd's 'office' then it truly was a joke of an office. There was the one chair there, as before. Apart from that it was bare, nothing but cobwebbed brickwork and stored props.

She wasn't entirely sure what had drawn her back, but something told her it was here she would find the final piece in the jigsaw of Todd's death. Amongst the people connected to the show, she'd seen secrets and plots and machinations. There was a play that some wanted to move to New York and others didn't. There was an actor with a limp he'd gained before his accident. There was Reuben Romano's hand clasped in Charlotte Webber's. And oddly, at the centre of it all, there was Brie Grebbson, a young woman with no personal stake in the play.

Diana was pondering this when a word on a packing box caught her eye. She moved towards it.

Grebbson.

It was written in untidy black marker but it was definitely the name: *Grebbson.*

Diana bent over to get a better look, noticing her shadow shift under the single bare bulb.

The box was soft, slightly damp with age. Diana pulled it open.

Inside there wasn't much. Just an old detachable

floppy disk drive and half a dozen empty thirty-five-millimetre film canisters. She hadn't seen canisters like that in years. There was a coiled power cable and a very small printer and, underneath that, a device that looked like a tiny television.

She lifted it out. There was a little screen on one side and a little lens on the other. She accidentally flicked a switch and an old-style USB connection attachment flicked out.

"Oh," Diana said. Things were starting to make sense.

It was an old digital video camera, the type from the nineties before people had started using phones for video.

It was almost an antique.

Diana called Zaf.

He picked up on the first ring.

"And you said young people don't use phones," she said.

"We receive calls, we don't make them. I'm currently up to my elbows in other people's rubbish."

"We're having fun," came Brie's voice.

"You're looking for a disk," said Diana. She looked at the camera. "A minidisc or a USB stick – no, too thick – or a flash card maybe. It's a storage thing."

"You sure?"

"It's video. You're looking for something that stores video."

"OK."

Zaf hung up. She hoped he'd got the message.

"Just what do you think you're doing in here?"

Diana spun round at the sound of the voice.

The doorman, Farrell Adesina, filled the doorway. His face was stern and his fists clenched.

Chapter Fifty

"It's a minidisc or something," Zaf told his bin-searching companions. "Something that stores video."

Brie nodded and started searching again, her gaze focused. Even Noah seemed to have got a second wind. He chuckled as he searched, clearly having a wonderful time.

Zaf sighed. This was important. Or at least, it was to Diana and to Brie.

And to whoever had broken into Brie's room.

He sifted through a pile of rubbish he'd hauled out of the bin, scanning for something that might fit Diana's description. It was hopeless.

He stood back. "What's a minidisc anyway?"

"I kind of remember them," said Noah, pulling

apart clumps of dust and hair as he searched. "They were like CDs I think, only, you know, mini."

"Uh-huh." Zaf set aside the clump of rubbish he'd been looking through. "Sounds pretty unreliable to me." *Easily lost. Easily stolen.* "I prefer the cloud."

"Everything is somewhere," said Brie. "Even in the cloud. Every song, every document, every recorded thing. It's stored somewhere."

"There was a time when music wasn't recorded," added Noah. "Go back more than a hundred, hundred and twenty years, and music only existed as words and notes on paper. And only *some* music at that. Music is the most ephemeral of arts."

"Ephemeral," said Zaf, savouring the word.

Noah rustled noisily through the rubbish.

"This is the bit where Noah explains that music makers are the most undervalued and hard-done-by creatives in the world," said Brie.

"Music is a living art form," Noah said, his tone terse. "It's not words on a page or paint on a canvas. It exists for a moment and then it dissipates into the air and is gone." He stood up, an object in his hand. "Ah."

Noah held out the object like it was delicate bird nestling in his palm. Zaf stepped towards him to get a better look.

In amongst the dusty strands of hair was a SD memory card. The kind you'd put in a computer or digital camera. It was bent, snapped in two straight down the middle.

Zaf felt his shoulders slump. "That was probably it, wasn't it?"

"Could be," said Brie. "I still don't know why Todd would be sending me a memory card."

"Do we keep looking?" Noah asked. "Maybe there's something else."

Zaf was sure this had been the thing they were looking for.

"I'll message Diana," he sighed.

Chapter Fifty-One

"You're in a lot of trouble," said Farrell.

"Me, Farrell?" Diana replied.

"You an' I might go back a long way. But I can only tolerate so much."

"Oh?" She let the old video camera drop back in the box.

He clicked his fingers and beckoned. "With me."

She did as she was told, more out of curiosity than fear of the doorman.

"A theatre's a like a ship, you know," he said as he led her down the corridor.

"I've heard that analogy before."

"It's a tightly run ship. Only stays afloat cos everyone does their job and everyone follows the rules."

"Oh, I have no problem with rules," Diana said.

He led her to a flight of stairs and they climbed up.

"Gareth Booncastle was limping this morning," she said.

Farrell looked back her, uninterested or not understanding.

"Just remembering," she added, "that you said you've broken a few legs in your time."

He shook his head. "Actors tell each other to break a leg all the time. Want to cast aspersions on them too, Diana?"

They were heading for the upper levels. Diana knew this route: they were on their way to the technical booth.

"Where are you taking me?" she asked.

Farrell said nothing. He opened the door to the technical booth and ushered her through. Diana watched his face, convinced that if she hadn't gone through voluntarily, he'd have shoved her.

The sound and lighting team were at their posts, following cues for the big number that ended the first act. The woman who'd been at the sound mixing desk last time was there again now. She looked round at Diana, her expression a mixture of amusement and contempt.

"Oh, here's one of them," she said.

"One of what?" said Diana.

The woman double-checked her desk and then glided on her wheeled chair over to a computer station.

"I just started recording," she said. "Remote cameras only."

She scrolled a cursor across the screen and clicked. A video started playing. Diana could see that it was from tonight's show. But the image wasn't of the stage.

"We record all manner of performances," the woman said. She slid back to the sound board to press a button, then returned to her screen.

Diana watched the footage of Newton crawling along the rows, shining a torch.

"That's your man, isn't it?" said Farrell.

"My man?" said Diana. "However you interpret that phrase, the answer's no. But yes, I know him."

"Words will be had," muttered Farrell.

"OK," she said. "I get it. He's in the way. You run a tight ship." She watched the edited video. "You seriously spent the night recording him?"

"A girl can get bored up here," said the sound woman. She clicked on the video and dragged it into a folder of other video files onscreen.

Diana pointed at the screen. "These are your files?"

"Yes."

"There's a lot of them."

A shrug. "Of course. All the raw feeds and then the files as they get edited together."

Diana nodded. "And you did the files for Todd previously."

"Yeah, I told you."

"Because he wanted them transferring?"

"Yes," the woman snapped. "I told you. Old format files transferred into a single file. Just some personal stuff. Not work stuff."

Diana could feel her heart rate picking up. "Because you get easily bored up here."

"Yep."

Diana waggled her finger at the screen. She tried to keep her voice casual. "And have you still got the raw files or the edited files or whatever for the stuff that Todd asked you to do?"

"Oi," said Farrell, "this isn't about anything else other than you and your man playing silly beggars in my theatre."

"Just... just give me a minute," Diana said. "Please. Do you have the files for Todd's thing?"

The sound engineer clicked to another window. "Sure. Lined up to be deleted, but yeah, they're here."

"And you haven't told anyone about these?"

The woman turned in her chair to look at Diana properly. "No one asked. Not you. Not the real cops."

"Play one. Please, play one."

The engineer sighed and double-clicked a file. It popped open.

It was a home video, a lounge or living room with glass doors overlooking a balcony and a grey London sky. In the foreground, a little girl, no more than five years old, danced around in a cheap yellow dress and a shiny plastic tiara.

"Just family stuff. Old," said the woman.

"Turn up the sound," whispered Diana. "Can you just turn up the sound for me?"

She leaned in, waiting.

The engineer adjusted a control and pulled out a headphone jack. Sound came from a speaker somewhere behind them, making Diana jump.

It wasn't loud, but it slapped into Diana like a bucket of cold water. The truth, confirmed in audio and video.

Farrell stepped back, confused.

"The old grey whistle test?" said Diana. "Did it pass, I wonder?"

"I don't get it," said the doorman. "It doesn't make sense."

"It makes perfect sense. It's why Todd had to die."

Chapter Fifty-Two

On the way back to the theatre, Zaf tried to wrap his head around what they'd been looking for. The broken memory card was important, surely. But why?

If it was linked to Todd's death, then whatever was on it might sabotage the deal. Or save it. He wasn't sure which.

Noah sat next to him on the tube, holding the broken card like it was a delicate baby animal. A kitten, maybe.

Zaf had spotted Newton before the performance, emerging from the bus with a can of tuna. Looking for Gus, still.

The bus was going to stink of tuna.

They came to their stop and Zaf stood up,

watching Noah cradling his precious object. Once broken, an SD card was effectively lost. Even Zaf knew that, and he'd never used the things.

Brie glanced at her phone as they emerged from the underground station into the lights of Piccadilly Circus.

"Final curtain has dropped," she said. "Serena will be wondering where I am."

Night had fallen and the statue of Eros glowed against the night, lit by spotlights from below.

Zaf's phone pinged: a text from Diana. "Diana says everyone's meeting in the bar. And the police have been called."

"Police?" said Noah.

Zaf shrugged. "I hope Newton hasn't been arrested." He'd been causing enough trouble, sneaking around the theatre. But during a performance?

They wove around the last of the theatregoers emerging from the Delphinium and made their way to the bar. Zaf could feel tension rising in his companions. What had Diana done that necessitated the presence of the police?

The long thin bar was filled with theatre folk, management, crew and those actors who were already out of costume. Gareth Booncastle sat on a bar stool, wincing most expressively and rubbing his leg as he sipped on a long drink. Zaf wondered if the police would be arriving soon.

Serena and Diana were standing beneath a television screen while one of the technical crew fiddled with a cable behind it.

"But what is it you have to show us?" asked Serena, exasperation lacing her voice.

"Something quite enlightening," Diana replied. "It explains everything."

"That doesn't answ—"

"Is this linked to the disruptions tonight?" asked Charlotte. "There was a man and a cat. It was like nothing I've ever seen."

The heavy-set doorman Zaf had encountered a few days ago was standing beside her. "I'm not sure," he said. "I barely understand it."

Diana turned to them both with a knowing look. "It will all make sense. And while what I'm about to show you will cause heartache, it will also explain Todd Granger's death."

A wave of murmurs swept through the group.

Serena narrowed her eyes at Diana. "You've solved his murder?"

"Yes," Diana replied. "Yes, I have." She looked past Serena and spotted Zaf. "Ah, our friends have returned with the evidence."

Zaf glanced at Noah. *The evidence?* The only evidence they had was broken. He opened his mouth to speak.

"For a time," Diana continued, "I thought this was

all about the Broadway deal. There seemed to be as many people keen to stop it as there were people anxious to see it go ahead." She surveyed the group. "If I've learned anything this week, it's that the theatre business is a precarious one, as likely to bring financial ruin as success."

"*Dick!*" shouted someone across the bar.

"Well, precisely," said Diana, shooting Zaf a look that reassured him, even though he wasn't entirely sure why. "And too much of my time was spent focused on Mr Romano here."

"Me?" The accountant placed a hand on his chest, his face paling.

She nodded. "You've been the odd one out all week, if I may say so. You're a relatively late addition to the American delegation, obviously not a well-travelled man—"

"I've travelled."

"Long weekends in Montauk, I recall. As a tourist, you've been a delight, a chance for me to re-see this city through innocent eyes. But your presence here has been a peculiarity, and the way you couldn't explain where you were on Wednesday morning during the time when Brie's hotel room was ransacked, led me—"

"You never told me your room had been ransacked." Serena glared at Brie.

"You're a busy woman." Brie shrugged. "And it was hardly ransacked."

"There was break-in," Diana said. "Things were moved. Searched through. And Mr Romano here couldn't explain where he was. His attempts to latch onto Gareth Booncastle for an alibi failed, as Brie recalled Gareth had an appointment elsewhere. It took me a while to realise what others could already see quite plainly." She gestured to Serena. "Reuben's your brother-in-law and, I recall, you suggested he was struggling with the notion that his marriage was over."

"I'm not struggling," Reuben complained.

"Oh, come on, man," said Serena. "Julietta said you'd been hanging around the neighbourhood with a look on your face like a kicked puppy."

Zaf looked at Reuben. He was staring back at Serena, no kicked puppy now.

"And a bit of travel has done him the world of good," said Diana. "A chance to meet new people, maybe even find new love."

Reuben glanced at Charlotte Webber. The theatre manager stepped almost imperceptibly closer to him, a smile flickering on her lips.

"I'm an idiot," Zaf whispered.

"Yeah?" Brie whispered back.

He gestured towards Reuben and Charlotte. "I saw them looking all secretive in the hotel that morning, and it never even occurred to me..."

"My own judgement was clouded," Diana continued, "by the fact that neither Mr Romano nor Mrs

Webber truly wanted the deal to go ahead. They seemed like ideal co-conspirators." She turned to look at Gareth. "Of course, they weren't the only ones who would have wanted to see the whole thing thwarted."

Gareth was looking down at his leg, rubbing it. He glanced up to see Diana's gaze on him, along with the rest of the group.

"What?" He winced as he shifted on his stool. "A ten-month stint on Broadway. An actor's dream, assuming I'm fit and well of course."

Zaf glanced at Brie, whose eyebrow was raised. There was something dodgy about Gareth Booncastle, alright. And it wasn't just his acting.

"I don't think there's anyone here," said Diana, "who isn't aware that you have your eyes on a bigger prize. I heard there were chats with a certain Mr Spielberg."

"The Wednesday morning appointment?" asked Serena.

"It wasn't Steven himself," said Gareth. "A friend of a friend of a friend."

"So he didn't break into my room," Brie said.

Diana looked at her. "We only have his word for it."

"Diana!" said Gareth, appalled.

"Oh, you are a gifted liar, Mr Booncastle. You've lied to us all day today. You're lying even now."

He puffed out his chest, his expression one of outrage. "I'll ha—"

Serena stepped forward. "This break-in. What was it for? What was stolen?"

"I didn't realise I'd lost anything," said Brie.

"Which is where Zaf, Brie and Noah have been this evening," said Diana. "The item at the heart of this is one of those little plastic memory card things. Todd sent it to the hotel the day he died and the hotel staff placed it in Brie's room in a little envelope or something."

Zaf thought of the envelopes Diana had picked up from Penny at reception. It was starting to make sense.

"How it ended up on the floor," Diana continued, "and then got sucked up by the cleaner's hoover – vacuum cleaner for our American friends – is something we'll probably never know."

Noah held up the broken SD card. "It was broken when we found it. So we'll never know what was on it, either."

Diana licked her lips. Were her eyes sparkling?

Zaf thought back to the last time she'd done this, when they'd accompanied a student group on a tour of the Houses of Parliament and a woman had been murdered. When he'd joined Chartwell and Crouch, he'd never known he was getting himself involved with an amateur sleuth.

"But what is most interesting about the break-in," Diana said, "is that Brie was far away while it happened. She was with Zaf on an errand in Piccadilly all morning."

Zaf exchanged glances with Brie. He felt his cheeks heat up. She gave him a *oops* smile.

"She had been sent away," said Diana. "Told to go and buy a bereavement gift for Todd Granger's family."

"It was Mrs Webber who sent her." Zaf pointed at Charlotte.

"I don't think so," said Charlotte.

"It was Serena who told me I should do it," Brie said.

"I was offering your services," said Serena airily.

Diana seemed unmoved by their suggestions. "Getting Brie out of the way allowed the perpetrator to explore her room without the risk of interruption."

"But what was on the little card?" asked Reuben.

"It was important to Todd," said Diana. "Even after he'd drunk a cocktail containing a lethal quantity of cocaine, even as his judgement was fading and his heart was racing towards an inevitable heart attack..."

She paused, surveying the group. All eyes were on her. Including Zaf's.

"Even then," she continued, "he went back up to the technical booth, spoke to the technicians, retrieved the card and asked them to send it to Brie at the hotel via the box office staff." Her voice lowered. "He was dying at that point, I think. If he'd not walked in a daze to the upper entrance to the lighting gantries and fallen over to his death, he would still have had that fatal heart attack sooner rather than later."

"We all knew he had a heart condition," said Noah. "And I wonder who here has access to cocaine?"

Diana nodded. "Absolutely. The drugs are Gareth Booncastle's, and they were used to kill Todd Granger."

Chapter Fifty-Three

Gareth's face was red. "What? You can't...! That's slanderous and—"

Diana continued, ignoring him. "But just as almost everyone knew Gareth was angling for a role in the next big Hollywood movie, nearly everyone knows Gareth has a drug habit."

"They do not!"

"Oh, they do," said Farrell.

"Let's hope Mr Spielberg's team don't have a problem with that," said Serena.

"Gareth knew his drugs had been used to spike Todd's cocktail," Diana said. "That day at the Londiniumarium, you clung to the detective chief inspector like a limpet. The questions you kept asking him. Would they be searching the theatre? Did they really need to keep poking around?"

"I play a detective on TV!" Gareth cried. "It was research!"

She shook her head. "Your habit has caused trouble before. In fact, don't you get your stunt double, Terry, to do little jobs for you? Todd was close to firing Farrell a while back for letting Terry slip by."

"Hey," said Farrell. "I didn't have nothin' to do with Mr Granger's death."

"I didn't say you did, Farrell, even if you have been known to break a leg or two in your time."

Gareth pointed at his leg. "This? This was a mudlarking injury. You all saw it. I have an appointment with a specialist in Harley Street on Saturday. If – and Lord above I hope not – if it's a significant injury then I might not be able to honour my commitments to the show going forward."

"You were limping before we went mudlarking," Diana said.

"I was not."

"You were. I saw you. You saw me see you, and you stopped."

For once, Gareth didn't have an answer.

Zaf stepped forward. "He'd already been hurt, but pretended he was fine until he could fake the injury later."

Diana twirled her fingers together. "It's the other way round."

"Oh, man," Brie sighed. "He's not hurt at all. The thing with the leg. It's all an act. When you saw him, he was just practising his limp before his big 'performance' by the Thames."

"I resent that remark," said Gareth.

Diana shrugged. "I'm sure a friendly doctor on Harley Street might be persuaded to attest to an injury that gets you out of your theatre contract. Which would allow you to accept any Hollywood offer that might be forthcoming."

Charlotte was staring at Gareth. "You... you're a disgrace."

"Miss Bakewell," said Serena, "you've done a very good job so far of telling us who did *not* kill Todd. While I'm enjoying your little show as much as everyone else, we were led to believe you'd tell us who *did* kill him."

"Yes. Quite." Diana turned to the sound engineer by the TV. They'd had a nice chat on the way down, and she'd discovered the woman's name.

"Tulip, are you ready to go?"

Tulip pressed a remote and the TV silently displayed a piece of home video footage.

Brie stared at the dancing girl in the yellow princess dress. "That's... that's me!"

"It's an old family video," Diana said. "Todd had found some old things of your dad's, maybe here, maybe somewhere else. A laptop, an old camera. That was his gift to you. He'd asked Tulip here to transfer it all to a more modern format."

"But the memory card...?" said Noah, still holding the broken piece of plastic in his hand.

Diana smiled. "The temporary files were on the computers upstairs. It was kind of you to search, but it turns out that was unnecessary."

"This was it?" said Brie. "Todd's gift to me? I mean, it's lovely, but I thought it would explain what happened to Todd."

"It does," said Diana. "I imagine what happened is that Todd didn't watch all the videos. Or at least, not with the sound turned up. Tulip?"

The sound woman turned up the volume.

Onscreen, the girl was singing in a distinctly childish tone: out of tune, but not caring. Offscreen, a piano played a heartfelt tune and a man's voice accompanied her. *Sparkling with mystery, a land of fantasy, where castles touch the sky, and wishes never die.*

The tune was catchy, both soaring and melodic. Diana watched as the group recognised it. Farrell was humming and tilting his head in time with the music.

"Wow, I remember this," said Brie.

"*Sparkling with majesty, my love, forever and always,*" Mitch sang.

"Sparkling with majesty," said Zaf. "Spark... *Voices of History*! This is the song Adele covered! From the musical!"

A dozen voices started shouting in agreement.

"*Superficially* similar," Noah conceded.

Diana looked at Tulip, who nodded. Another video replaced the first.

Mitch played, just his legs and part of his face visible behind a baby grand piano, and Brie sang along.

"*London's Changing!*" someone shouted.

"What is this?" Charlotte's lip was trembling.

Diana turned to her. "It's like Serena says. All art is plagiarism. Isn't that right, Noah?"

Heads swivelled towards the songwriter.

He was still clutching the SD card. "Mitch and I *might* have collaborated on a few tu—"

"Back when you were 'student princes of song and dance'?" said Diana. "That's what you said when I found you in Todd's 'office' smashing up an old laptop. Mitch's old laptop, I'd wager. And at that moment you offered to confess something to me." She laughed. "The musical. The plot. It's your... oh, what's that stupid word Zaf used?"

"FessHole," said Zaf.

She looked at him, returning his encouraging smile. "FessHole. Jack Ha'penny, a struggling artist who finds a box of another artist's work and passes it off as his own, but only for the greater good."

"I just wanted to keep Mitch's songs alive," Noah said. "It's not stealing." He turned to Brie. "I did it out of love. He was a wonderful songwriter, your dad. We worked on so many things together." He pulled back his shoulders, his gaze traversing the group. "Who's to say that I didn't create those songs, and Mitch just embellished them to entertain little Brie?"

"That car crash of a musical over the road might say otherwise," said Charlotte. "I'm guessing you ran out of Mitch's songs to recycle for *Dick!*"

"Musically, you were nothing without him," said Gareth.

"You can talk," said Noah, gesturing at Gareth's leg. "You with yo—"

"And suddenly," said Diana, "having sunk too much of your own money into that failure of a musical, protecting your own interests became more important than anything else."

Zaf was frowning. "Charlotte never asked Brie or anyone to get a bereavement hamper."

"Who ever heard of a bereavement hamper, honestly?" said Charlotte.

Zaf pointed at Noah. "You came in and asked about Brie's room. It was you that mentioned a 'gift', but you said it was Charlotte's idea. And then Brie picked up on that and asked what gift, and suddenly out of nowhere it became a posh hamper and morphed into the perfect excuse to get rid of Brie. It was very convenient, but you never meant the conversation to go that way. You were talking about Todd's gift to Brie. You were the one in the room!"

"Why do you think he was so keen to go with you tonight?" Diana said. "Was it Noah who found the 'broken' memory card."

Zaf's mouth dropped open. Brie nodded.

"You broke it yourself," Zaf said to Noah.

"I don't think we can just go around making things up," said Noah.

"Noah, did you kill Todd?" Brie's voice was hoarse.

Noah pulled back. "Kill? I didn't want to kill him, as such."

Realising what he'd said, he staggered away, his mouth agape.

"You know how you sometimes enter the room at the perfect moment?" came a voice.

Diana turned to see DCI Clint Sugarbrook draping his trenchcoat over his arm as he walked into the bar.

She smiled.

"Stunning entrance," Gareth Booncastle agreed.

Chapter Fifty-Four

Diana and Zaf strolled from the Delphinium towards the underground station at Piccadilly Circus.

"So, what d'you think'll happen now?" Zaf asked.

"Apart from Noah Dart having some difficult questions to answer from the police?" She shrugged. "There's no physical evidence he killed Todd. I suppose in all the confusion he took the incriminating glass and just washed it or something. But then again, Carmen at the hotel should be able to identify him as the man who went into Brie's room. Circumstantial, I grant."

Zaf frowned. "I mean about the play, the songs."

Diana's face was caught in the glow of a dozen theatre billboards. She stopped walking and looked at him. The light picked out the silken threads of the top she wore under her velvet jacket.

"I suppose Brie or her mum might be on the phone to their lawyers," she said. "They're the true heirs to Mitch Grebbson's work. And I guess the Delphinium, or the investors behind it, will be doing likewise." She carried on walking. Zaf hurried to keep up. He suddenly realised he was tired.

"If everyone is sensible," she continued, "then I'd imagine large amounts of money are about to change hands. Earnings which had been claimed by Noah and should have rightly gone to Mitch's family can be diverted to their proper destination. The musical is still viable, the songs are still cracking tunes. It's funny how a musician like Noah could only find success by stealing Mitch's work."

"Like Eros and Anteros." Zaf pointed at the aluminium statue of the winged god at the centre of Piccadilly Circus.

"Sorry?"

"Eros, unable to grow and thrive without the selfless love of his brother, Anteros. The statue is technically of Anteros, not Eros."

"Since when were you the expert on all things London?"

He winked. "I've been learning."

She raised an eyebrow.

They walked in silence for five minutes or so, making their way along the edge of Green Park towards the Victoria Memorial. Zaf liked this route: at night it was quiet, and he could almost forget he was in one of the world's busiest cities.

As they passed the front of Buckingham Palace, Diana spoke.

"Eros and Anteros. They've made me think."

"Yes?"

"Do you think you and I can learn to live together?"

Zaf pushed down a *no*.

"I don't know. I hate the fact that I annoy you. I don't want to argue with you. I feel bad that I owe you so much, but I also hate constantly feeling like I'm walking on eggshells."

"Walking on eggshells? Really? Is that what we're calling it when I express concern that you've lost a box of cannabis-filled brownies?"

Diana looked at him with irritation for a moment, then softened.

"Sorry," she said. "Fine. Yes, we can do better than this. Maybe one day we'll feel emotionally strong enough to read the secrets in our so-called FessHole."

They approached Grosvenor Place and the larger theatres around Victoria. Sparkling advertisements rose up around them.

"What do we do, then?" said Zaf. "I feel like you want me to leave but I don't know where I can go."

"I don't want you to leave."

He took a deep breath. "Good. Cos I can't actually afford to move out."

"We need to try harder to respect each other's feelings," she said.

"Yeah." He looked down at his feet as they walked. They'd passed the theatres now and were navigating the crowds around the bus station. "How do we do that, though? I know what I'm like. I'll agree to everything now, but by tomorrow I'll have forgotten half of it."

And Diana would be pleasant now, but annoyed with him as soon as he reminded her she didn't have the flat to herself any more. He didn't say as much, though.

Diana nodded. "We need a physical reminder, or something we can point to when needed."

"Like a friendship contract, I've seen those. We make one and stick it to the fridge."

"Sounds the kind of thing teenage girls would have."

"Maybe there are versions for grown-ups." Were there?

"I'd be happy to try it," Diana said. They'd turned along a side street and her heels echoed against the fronts of the houses. "What kind of thing goes in there? Are there standard ones or do we make our own?"

Zaf tried to picture it. "Bullet points. A list of stuff we agree to. We can decide on our own list. So... for example, we agree to listen to each other."

"Always?" Diana frowned. "Maybe we nominate a particular time of day when we have to pay special attention to what the other person is saying."

"That could work."

"We should have something that stops us bottling up minor niggles," she said. "We need a point on the contract to say we should bring up any minor issues at the earliest opportunity, and that we discuss them in an adult manner."

Zaf smiled. It wasn't just him trying to make this work. That was good.

"Be open and adult about minor niggles," he said. "Got it. These are all about communication really, aren't they?"

"It is at the heart of most things."

"What about something more generic, like we should have each other's back?" he suggested.

She eyed him. "OK."

"Shouldn't we write these down?"

"I have an excellent memory." She tapped the side of her head.

"I've noticed that. Your capacity for names and faces, and just remembering those little things people say."

She smiled. "It makes me who I am."

They turned the corner into Eccleston Square. Zaf was looking forward to his bed. Not that he'd ever admit that to anyone.

"And you're good," he said.

"Good at what?" Diana stopped on the bottom step of their house and looked at him.

"Just good." He smiled. "A good person."

She laughed dismissively. "I wouldn't be so sure. Everyone has a few skeletons in their closet."

"No," he disagreed. "You're possibly too good."

She narrowed her eyes for a moment, then turned to open their front door. Zaf could see Alexsei silhouetted in the hallway light. Maybe he'd tell the landlord that Diana was good, too. It would give the two of them something to agree on.

Read a free story, Gus the Theatre Cat

Gus the tabby cat is now a firm fixture at Chartwell and Crouch Bus Tours. Newton the bus driver has taken him under his wing and regularly provides him with cans of tuna. And the tour guides Diana and Zaf are finding he's a hit with the guests.

But then when Diana and Zaf are showing a group of theatre professionals around London, Gus disappears in a West End theatre.

Newton is distraught. He's searched the theatre high and low but can't find his beloved feline friend.

One night, when Diana and Zaf are watching the performance, he has a plan. It involves plenty of cunning, a fair amount of sneaking around in the auditorium and quite a lot of tinned tuna.

Can Newton find Gus without causing total chaos for the audience?

Find out in this London Cozy Mysteries short story.

Read *Gus the Theatre Cat* for FREE at rachelm clean.com/gus.

Read the London Cozy Mysteries Series

Death at Westminster, London Cozy Mysteries Book 1

Death in the West End, London Cozy Mysteries Book 2

Death on Tower Bridge, London Cozy Mysteries Book 2

...and more to come

Buy now in ebook or paperback.

Also by Rachel McLean

The DI Zoe Finch Series – Buy now in ebook, paperback and audiobook

Deadly Wishes, DI Zoe Finch Book 1

Deadly Choices, DI Zoe Finch Book 2

Deadly Desires, DI Zoe Finch Book 3

Deadly Terror, DI Zoe Finch Book 4

Deadly Reprisal, DI Zoe Finch Book 5

Deadly Fallout, DI Zoe Finch Book 6

Deadly Christmas, DI Zoe Finch Book 7

Deadly Origins, the FREE Zoe Finch prequel

The Dorset Crime Series – Buy now in ebook, paperback or audiobook

The Corfe Castle Murders, Dorset Crime Book 1

The Clifftop Murders, Dorset Crime Book 2

The Island Murders, Dorset Crime Book 3

The Monument Murders, Dorset Crime Book 4

The Millionaire Murders, Dorset Crime Book 5

The Fossil Beach Murders, Dorset Crime Book 6

The Blue Pool Murders, Dorset Crime Book 7

Also by Millie Ravensworth

The Cozy Craft Mysteries – Buy now in ebook and
paperback

The Wonderland Murders

The Painted Lobster Murders

The Sequinned Cape Murders

The Swan Dress Murders

The Tie-Dyed Kaftan Murders

The Scarecrow Murders